MARINA OLIVER

COURTESAN OF THE SAINTS

Complete and Unabridged

LINFORD
Leicester

First published in Great Britain in 1976

First Linford Edition
published 2002

British Library CIP Data

Oliver, Marina, *1934* –
    Courtesan of the Saints.—Large print ed.—
Linford romance library
1. Love stories
2. Large type books
I. Title
823.9'14 [F]

ISBN 0–7089–9775–9

Published by
F. A. Thorpe (Publishing)
Anstey, Leicestershire

Set by Words & Graphics Ltd.
Anstey, Leicestershire
Printed and bound in Great Britain by
T. J. International Ltd., Padstow, Cornwall

This book is printed on acid-free paper

1

'The Devil himself must be rubbing his hands with glee to witness this display of sinfulness amongst his enemies!'

Miles Talbot, who had been leaning against the wainscot chatting with his friend Robert Peyton, turned round. The words had been muttered close to his ear, so that he expected to discover that they had been addressed to him. The only person near enough to have given expression to such thoughts, however, was turned away from Miles, and all he could see was a sober black suit and a close cropped grey head.

Miles glanced back in some amusement at Robert, but his friend had not heard the remark and was continuing his own discourse. Miles shrugged, and transferred his attention back to Robert. He was not to be left alone.

'God in His righteousness will punish the evil doers!'

This prophecy had been uttered in a louder voice and Robert heard it, and grinned at Miles, raising his eyebrows.

'Your first Saint,' he whispered softly, and Miles nodded slightly as he turned to the man behind him.

This time the sober suited one was facing Miles, and viewed him with intense displeasure. Miles noted the thin straggly hair receding from a narrow brow, pale grey eyes that matched the hair, and a gaunt face, with pale, unhealthy skin stretched taut across prominent bones, apart from where there were deep lines of displeasure round the nose and mouth.

The frown deepened as this individual looked back at Miles, noting the long curling locks, the width and strength of the shoulders under the brocade coat, and the wide lace collar and cuffs adorning it.

'Were you addressing your remarks to me, sir?' Miles enquired courteously.

'Aye, and to any of them that can hear, when they are not deafened by the seductive screeches of the fiddles!'

'Did you not appreciate the entertainment?' Miles asked, raising his eyebrows.

' 'Tis an invitation to lewdness! Men should have a better care for God's wrath than to tempt the Devil with such trumpery entertainments that do them no good.'

'Would you ban all music?' Robert asked, and received a fanatical glare from the prophet.

'Aye, along with many other of the wicked temptations that abound, and that are seen here, even in this godly house!'

'Have a care, neighbour,' interrupted another man seated nearby, who had overheard the conversation.

'Why indeed should I have a care? Are you threatening me? Or insinuating that I am afraid?'

The newcomer to the conversation laughed. 'No, indeed, Faithful! No one who knows you would ever accuse you of timidity or dare to threaten you. I but point out to you that you are in danger of insulting our hostess if you condemn her entertainments in such fashion.'

The man addressed as Faithful pursed his lips, and drew himself up to his full height, still scarcely reaching Miles' shoulder.

'I say no word against that gracious lady! You malign me to read such into my remarks. Mistress Weston is pure and innocent, and as such too like to be led astray by evil counsellors!'

'Come, Faithful. There is nought sinful in a gathering such as this, where we but eat and drink and talk, and listen to a little music!'

' 'Tis an occasion of sin,' Faithful asserted stubbornly. 'We are told that such merrymaking, the wearing of indecorous clothing, and immoderate laughter, lead only too easily to sinful thoughts, and from them 'tis a simple step to sinful actions, both hateful in the eyes of God and all godly men.'

'I wonder then that you venture yourself into such danger!'

'You scoff, Dick Ashford, but your sins will be noted and you will in good time be punished for them.'

'No doubt,' Dick Ashford agreed amiably. 'But I would prefer that you do not accuse Mistress Weston of providing occasions of sin!'

'She is unaware of the dangers, she is so pure and untouched herself.'

'I do not think you need to concern yourself on her behalf.'

'She has no one else to warn her. These folks who take so lavishly of her hospitality, her generosity, they do not care that they may be guiding her into wicked ways. You taunt me for venturing myself, but I am in no danger. I will not fall from the path of righteousness. I but seek to aid others who are in danger from the ungodly company that they are forced to keep!'

With a fierce glare at Ashford, and then a scowl at Miles and Robert, he swung round and stumped away to the far side of the large room, and Ashford chuckled gently to himself.

Miles looked across the room to where the hostess they had been discussing, whom Faithful was so anxious to save, was talking animatedly to others of her guests.

Mistress Weston was a tall woman, fair skinned and dark haired. Miles guessed her age to be early twenties. She had large dark eyes that had appraised him frankly when he had first been introduced to her earlier in the evening. He could see now the dark lashes curling onto her delicately shaped cheeks, and the full mouth that he had wanted to kiss the instant he had set eyes on it. She was wearing a simple dark blue gown with moderate amounts of lace at the cuffs and neck, and it could not have been called indecorous. But the way she wore it, so that it displayed her full breasts and narrow waist, and suggested supple limbs beneath the full skirts, could well,

Miles conceded, distract men into sinful thoughts.

He was not allowed to indulge in them for long,

'Methinks we have not met before? Allow me to introduce myself. Dick Ashford's the name.'

Miles turned to him with a smile lingering on his lips.

'Miles Talbot. Your service, sir.'

'I have seen you here before,' Ashford went on, turning to Robert.

'Indeed yes, I come to visit Mistress Weston whenever the opportunity arises. I remember you, but we were not introduced. There were far more people here on that occasion. Robert Peyton, sir.'

'You cannot come often, or I would have met you before.'

'Unfortunately not. My estates are in the west, and I do not come to London more than once or twice a year.'

'And you, Mr. Talbot?'

'I have but recently returned from the Low Countries. I have been in the armies there for some years.'

'Indeed? Then we must compare notes. I was until recently a Colonel in the New Model. What campaigns were you in?'

'I was engaged for most of the time in Flanders. But after we captured Hulst, there was little fighting. I was unwilling to join either France or Spain at that time, and remained in Holland, but the situation in this last year between the States and England caused me to return here.'

'You did well. If you have a mind for more, we could use your experience in the Army here.'

'I thank you. To be honest, I have had enough of the army life.'

'Aye, you seem to feel as I do. There is little excitement or chance of advancement in the army now.'

'I was hoping to buy a small estate. I have some small inheritance, and intend to look around me.'

'Well, if I can be of any assistance, should you change your mind, I will speak for you to one of our commanders.'

'You appear to have much influence.'

'The Colonel has other tasks now, in Parliament,' Robert put in.

'Indeed? You are in this new Parliament then?' Miles queried.

'I have indeed been so honoured by being called upon to help govern the country.'

' 'Tis an unhappy country in many ways, since the rebellion.'

'Aye, and the inefficient Parliaments we have had to suffer have made it worse.'

'The General was supported by most people then, when he dissolved the Rump? Forgive my ignorance, but I have been so long away from English affairs, I know only the merest details and nought of the truth of matters.'

'The General will ensure for us good government. This present Parliament was selected by him and the Council. We know what needs to be done, and intend to do our duty.'

Miles nodded. 'From the little I have seen of you, Colonel, I feel confident that England is in good hands.'

The Colonel bowed graciously. 'We could do with some purging, I will confess,' he said, glancing across the room.

Miles followed his glance, and saw that Faithful was standing aloof from the rest of the company, glowering at them.

'You mean our recent friend?' Robert asked.

'Surely he is not of your company in Parliament?' Miles said in surprise.

'Unfortunately, yes.'

'Who is he?'

'His name is Denham. Dare-to-be-faithful-to-God Denham. Usually known as Faithful.'

Miles grinned. 'I wondered at the appellation. I thought it might have some earthly connection.'

'Not so. I believe he was named

10

Francis by his parents, but no one has ever known him as aught other than Faithful.'

'How comes he to be selected by the General?'

'He needs to gain the support of the City for his new measures, and Faithful, though he does not look it, is an exceedingly wealthy man. He is one of the Skinners' Company, and that is one of the most influential Companies in the City.'

'I see. What does he here, though?'

'He seeks to turn others from sin! You heard him declare that was his object!'

Miles laughed. 'Is he serious? One of the Elect?'

'I do not in truth think he is concerned with me, or with you. No, 'tis the attractions of our hostess draws him, like a moth to a candle.'

Robert smiled. 'Even such as he,' he murmured. 'Did I not promise you that Mistress Weston was greatly to be admired?' he asked Miles.

'You did indeed. I grant that she is all you say of her.'

Dick Ashford nodded. 'There are few to compare with Mistress Weston. She is beautiful and charming, and an accomplished hostess.'

'She entertains a great deal?' Miles asked curiously.

'Indeed yes. She is generous, and extends her friendship to many, even such undeserving boors as Faithful Denham. There are gatherings here most evenings, sometimes just a few friends, sometimes a goodly number, as tonight, and on occasion so many that one can scarce move through the rooms for the crush!'

Miles looked across the room at the object of their conversation. She was moving about competently amongst her guests, unobtrusively making sure that they all were supplied with the plentiful food and wine, and were not neglected. As Miles watched, she moved away from one group, throwing a laughing remark over her shoulder, then moved to Faithful Denham's side.

He was apparently surly. Miles could distinguish his frowns and imagine the protestations that he was making. Dick Ashford's attention had been claimed by another guest, and Miles was free to watch the woman, who was indeed little more than a girl, gradually charm the ill humour out of Denham's face, and then lead him over to a small group of men and women who were seated round a table talking earnestly. Leaving him there, she circulated again, and Miles stood watching, leaning back against the wall, knowing that she would eventually approach him.

Cherry Weston was conscious that she was performing her duties as hostess somewhat mechanically that evening. She was tense, and found it unusually difficult to concentrate on what her guests were saying to her. She smiled and praised, asked interested questions about their families and friends, exchanged gay quips with the younger ones, pressed them to take

13

more wine, or sample some of the many dishes laid out for them, but all the time she knew that she was performing. It was with great difficulty that she drove the image of a young man's face from her mind.

When she found a moment that was not occupied with attending her guests, she allowed her thoughts to wander back, and wondered why that image, which had not recently troubled her, should be so insistent that evening.

There were not many such moments. She moved round the room, taking care not to offend any guests by ignoring them, or spending too little time with them, and eventually, with a quickening of her heartbeats, approached Robert and Miles.

'I hope you find our little gathering to your taste, Mr. Talbot?' she said, smiling up at him, then turned a little hastily to Robert.

'And you, my friend? How are things with you? Your wife? When are you going to bring her to see me again? We enjoyed our meetings last year enormously.'

'I would have brought Jane, but she is breeding, and has been advised to stay at home.'

'Oh, give her my very best wishes. I do hope that this time you have a son!'

'I will tell Jane, and she will do her best to satisfy your wishes!'

'Do so! Mr. Talbot, do you know Robert's wife?'

'I have not yet met her.'

'She is delightful, he is the most fortunate man alive to have her. I do not know how he can bear to leave her, but I will be selfish, and say I am pleased he did so, for he brought you here.'

Miles looked at her, and after a while smiled, an intimate smile deep into her eyes. With an effort she broke her gaze away from his, and laughed a little breathlessly.

'I hope you will come here again, when Robert has deserted us to return to Jane. He never remains long enough in London. But you will be welcome here. Do you stay long?'

Miles shrugged. 'I have made no definite plans as yet.' He smiled again. 'But I will most decidedly accept your kind invitation and visit you again.'

After a few more general remarks, Mistress Weston left them and passed on to others of her guests, leaving Miles to chat with some of the younger men Robert had introduced him to. It was growing late, and soon the guests began to make their farewells.

The older people went first, apart from Faithful Denham, who lingered until only a few others remained. Then, seeming to despair of his vigil, he left in a great hurry, sparing his hostess but a few words as he went.

Robert and Miles were almost the last to go, with another pair of young men. Ashford was still there, but shook his head slightly when Robert asked if they were going in the same direction and was rising from the settle where he had been sitting only as the others left the room.

Mistress Weston bade them all farewell, and laughingly declared that she expected them to be at her next gathering a few days hence. It came to Miles' turn to speak with her.

'When shall I come back?' he asked softly.

She looked quickly across at Ashford, then smiled brightly.

'I shall be here tomorrow evening, if that is not too soon for you to come again,' she answered quietly. 'It has been my pleasure to meet you,' she went on in a louder voice, and Miles nodded, then turned away.

Later that evening, Cherry tossed restlessly in bed, unable to sleep. The face she had been refusing to see in her thoughts was now allowed to emerge from whatever regions it had been banished to, but it was overlaid by another face, that of the newcomer to her house, Miles Talbot.

She struggled with her confused thoughts, her memories, and her present and past feelings. This man was so very like that old, long lost love of hers, that her emotions on seeing him had distracted her all the evening and now most of the night. Even while Dick had been with her she had thought of them both, the young Harry and the older Miles confused in her thoughts.

She forced herself to compare them calmly. This man was much taller than Harry, almost half a head so. And his eyebrows, with a slight quirk that gave him a laughing expression, were not the same as Harry's straight thick ones. They had the same vivid blue eyes, but Harry's face was rounder. It was after all a superficial resemblance. Why then, had the man Talbot brought back the memory of Harry so intensely? She had not thought of him romantically for many years now. Why should she be so bedevilled by thoughts of him now, induced by a stranger?

She wondered who the stranger was. Not a country friend of Robert Peyton's, that she was certain of. But he

18

had not seemed to know any of the other people there. Why had he come? And why had he made such immediate use of the invitation she had extended to him? It could simply be that he was attracted by her beauty. Or he might be an adventurer searching for a rich widow. She had met many of both kinds. Yet some instinct told her that there was some deeper reason. She determined to make enquiries about him.

Having decided on this, her thoughts drifted back to Harry, and the time, nearly ten years ago, when they had been so happy together planning their lives. It was a long time since she had railed against the cruel fate that had parted them when her parents had refused to consider him, despite his knighthood, and preferred the rich James Weston instead. If only she had been allowed to marry him, she would have been leading such a vastly different life now.

Giving way to one of her rare moods

of despondency, she reviewed her life, and wondered what there was still in store for her. At length, as the dawn crept through the cracks in the shutters, she fell asleep, tears on the long lashes, and the image of Harry and Miles in her mind.

2

Miles and Robert left Mistress Weston's large house in Canning Street, and turned westwards to walk towards the crumbling building that used to be the Cathedral of St. Paul's, and was now used for a multitude of unhallowed purposes.

When they reached their lodgings in nearby Cheapside, Robert poured wine, and they sat down. They had spoken but a few words since leaving the house.

'You succeeded in establishing your interest with the lady, then, Miles. Good work. I could at times wish for your skill!'

Miles laughed. 'What, and the faithful Jane waiting for you at home?'

'Merely in the way of duty, I hasten to add! But you are free to enjoy yourself. Do not be too carried away by her charms and forget what you are here to do.'

'I promise you that will not happen, Robert. No woman has sufficient charms to deflect me. But in all seriousness, do you think she will be worth cultivating?'

'You saw the gathering tonight! And met at least two members of the Barebones Parliament. There will be others. Knowing Cherry Weston is one of the best ways to get to know them.'

'Tell me about her. I am curious.'

'I thought you would be.' Robert chuckled.

'That sort of curiosity I can satisfy by myself! Her history, where does she come from? How is't that she behaves as she does, defying the conventions of men like Faithful, and still holding them her slaves?'

'Did you not feel her charm, her power over men?'

'Too well! But what lies behind it?'

'Her father was a wealthy wool merchant in Norwich. He married a girl from the lesser nobility, who was penniless and determined that neither she nor her family would ever be in need again.'

'Are they still alive?'

'The father died some years back and her mother remarried, another wealthy merchant in Bristol.'

'Was she as attractive as Cherry?'

'Oh, yes. She is over forty now, but still at the height of her beauty, and looking no more than thirty.'

'Cherry was the only child?'

'The only girl to survive. She has a brother a year older, who continues his father's business in Norwich.'

'So she did not inherit her father's wealth?'

'Only a small part of it. But that was enough to make her a suitable match for James Weston, who was more than twice her age, but a very wealthy man, one of the Mercers' Company, and on the lookout for a young wife to bear him sons to follow in his business. He had just lost his second wife, and had yet no children when he went courting Cherry.'

'Was she more successful in giving them to him?'

'No. They were married in fortyfour, when Cherry was just fourteen, but her elderly husband, who was then over forty, was more eager for military glories than for his child wife's embraces. Soon after the marriage he was with the army at Marston Moor, having left his shop to his younger brother's care.'

'When did he die? Was he killed in battle?'

'Yes, but not until six years later at Dunbar. In between his campaigns he spent a good deal of time with his wife, whose beauty eclipsed that of her mother.'

'So she has been widowed for three years. A long time.'

'You think it strange that she does not remarry?'

'There must have been plenty of opportunity for her, rich as well as beautiful. I assume she is rich?'

'Exceedingly. Mayhap you have found the reason. She was not, I believe, happy in her marriage, and the only time I saw Weston I loathed him on sight. I could not blame her for relishing her freedom and keeping control of her fortune. She is well capable of seeing to it herself.'

'What was he like?'

'A brute of a man, used to giving orders and having them obeyed instantly, even by his so delightful wife. But she would not obey him always. There were rumours that he beat her nigh to death when she was but fifteen, and wed but a year.'

'How did you meet them?'

'About four years ago, when I was betrothed to Jane. She lived in Bristol and her family know Cherry's mother. Cherry and Weston were visiting them, and we met. Two years ago Jane and I came to London and called to see Cherry, who had been widowed the previous year. I now see her whenever I am in London, and she visited us in Somerset last year.'

'But despite her husband, she still remains friends with his acquaintances?'

'She has a much wider circle than ever he had, but yes, many of the City merchants and their wives visit her, and also many of the army officers. Cromwell himself has dined with her, and she is on friendly terms with his daughter Elizabeth.'

'Are many of her friends like Faithful?'

'Quite a few. 'Tis amazing how she endures their ranting, for 'tis undoubtedly not to her taste. Also I find it amazing that she can persuade them to condone in her what they would instantly condemn in other women. Her dress, the constant entertaining, her gaiety. It must drive those like Faithful to distraction, but she charms her way through all disapproval!'

Miles laughed. 'All men are alike in bed, whatever they wear out of it!'

'I doubt whether she has entertained Faithful in bed!'

'I suspect that is the reason for his glumness. Could you not see the desire in his eyes?'

'But he is one of the Saints!' Robert was aghast at the very thought. 'He preaches nearly every week. I went once out of curiosity, and what I could understand of his ravings, which I confess was very little, was all to do with the dire punishments for those who fornicated!'

'He will not admit his lust, would be horrified to recognise it, but 'tis there, eating into him. He must satisfy his cravings by railing against those who dare what he does not,' Miles suggested.

Robert considered this. 'There is something in that,' he agreed.

'I shall commiserate with him. But there are others who frequent the house?'

'Many,' Robert reassured him. 'If you gain Cherry's friendship, which seems to have been achieved already, you will be welcome there at any time and will have ample opportunity to meet them and cultivate them, and through them get to know others of their persuasions.'

Miles was silent for a while and drank his wine, then poured out another glass.

'I am most grateful to you for introducing me to them. It was otherwise going to be difficult to infiltrate their ranks, but now I will be accepted, and the time saved may be all important.'

'Are you hoping simply to gain information?'

'More than that. We will find it very useful to discover how much they know of our activities. But apart from that, we wish to know which men in positions of authority might be sympathetic to the idea of restoration. The King, unlike some of his advisers, is willing to explore any way of recovering the throne. If it can be done by armed rebellion, then he will agree to that, but

after the experiences of two years sinc
he is somewhat dubious of the amoun
of support that is like to achieve.'

'That was when he came at the head
of a foreign army!' Robert protested.
'Many Englishmen resented that.'

'What matters the means? He would
try a foreign army again if there were a
chance of success. But he would, I
know, prefer that he were restored by
the many rather than the few, if only to
avoid possible disputes afterwards. That
is why I am here, in the hopes of
discovering those of different parties
who could be drawn together in his
support.'

'I do not think many of our presen
rulers are like to welcome a restore
monarchy. A concerted rising in man
parts of the country is the be
opportunity.'

'That may come. You concentrate
that part of it, and I will do this. Af
all, with Mistress Cherry around, I sh
have some enjoyment at it!'

'I wish you joy.'

The following day Miles saw Robert start off on his long ride to Somerset, and spent the day wandering round the City, renewing his acquaintance with it after an absence of more than four years.

He decided not to appear too eager to be at Mistress Weston's house that evening, and did not arrive until very close to the usual hour for supper. He was shown into a small parlour overlooking a garden at the back of the house. The maid told him that Mistress Weston begged that he would excuse her for her tardiness, but she would be down as soon as possible.

He smiled, mentally applauding Cherry for her victory in this first round, and stood looking out of the window until she came into the room.

Turning, he narrowed his eyes as he saw her. She was dressed in white, with the bodice cut low and tight fitting, laced with gold ribbons. A gold underpetticoat was visible where her skirts were looped back, and she offered

tantalising glimpses of scarlet slippers as she moved forwards to greet him. The only jewel she wore was a ruby pendant, which rested provocatively in the hollow between her breasts, just above her bodice.

She smiled warmly at him.

'I do regret I was not ready in time to welcome you. 'Tis most remiss of me, and I beg your pardon. Will you forgive me?'

'I would be churlish indeed to grumble at so slight a delay, when you present such a charming vision as a result of it!'

She raised her brows. 'You are a flatterer, sir. But I will not keep you from your supper any longer. Come, let us go into the dining parlour.'

He gave her his arm, and she led him through the door at the far side of the room from the one he had entered by. Beyond was another small room, with a small table set for two. A large side table held numerous dishes, and a young manservant stood waiting to serve them.

'I prefer to entertain here when I have just one or two friends,' she explained to him, as they sat down. 'I call it the dining parlour, and the other, why, 'tis almost a banqueting hall! I feel lost in it when I am alone. I trust you do not object to the informality.'

'Indeed no, I am delighted at the opportunity of seeing more of your delightful house. The parlour I saw yesterday was most impressive, excellent for such as yesterday's gathering.'

'But a little overpowering for just the two of us. We will sit in my special parlour afterwards. I am always most at my ease there.'

'I cannot imagine you ill at ease in any situation, Mistress Weston,' Miles rejoined.

She smiled her thanks at the compliment, and they chatted easily throughout the meal. He complimented her on the excellence of the food and wine, and brought the conversation round to the previous evening, when she had provided similarly excellent refreshments. He was able to ask her questions about the guests, and she told him amusing anecdotes about many of them. He responded by stories of his life in the army, but neither of them volunteered much information about themselves.

They did not lack for conversation, as both of them were skilled at entertaining, and the meal passed delightfully quickly. The servant withdrew, and Cherry ushered Miles through yet another door connecting that room with another, more of a boudoir than a parlour.

It was very feminine in style, with upholstered chairs, and many cushions. Miles wandered across to inspect a miniature portrait hanging beside the door to yet a further room. It was of a woman very like Cherry, but in a dress of twenty years before.

'Who is this?' he asked, turning back to her.

'My mother, when she was my age.'

Cherry came to stand beside him.

'She is beautiful.'

'Yes, indeed, and she is still so.' Cherry laughed. 'Only a few months ago we were taken for sisters. I do not believe she will ever grow old.'

'You are going to follow in her footsteps, and because you are ten times as beautiful now, you will stay like it till you are a hundred!'

Cherry laughed. 'Fie, sir, what an extravagant compliment.'

'Are you bored with being told that you are so lovely?'

'No, indeed! What woman would be?'

'Some women would deny it, protest boredom, while angling for yet more declarations.'

'I hope I am not like other women,' she said, wrinkling up her nose at him.

He laughed. 'The first sign of vanity I have detected in you! No, indeed, you far surpass all your sisters.'

He lifted her hand and kissed it, looking all the while into her eyes. Then he pulled her towards him, and

unresisting she came into his arms. He could feel the rising excitement in his own blood, and sensed it also in her. He kissed her gently at first, then more urgently, and she responded with equal passion.

When they were breathless, he lifted his head and looked without speaking into her eyes. A slight raising of his eyebrows, and with one accord they were moving towards the door which led, as Miles had expected, into a luxuriously furnished bedroom.

The candle was already lit beside the bed, and it shed a soft glow round the room. The covers were turned down, and soft rugs covered the floor.

Cherry was unresisting as Miles moved towards the bed. In silence, he expertly set about the task of removing her gown. It was all she wore, and was soon cast aside. Her body was all he had imagined it to be, smooth and supple, slim yet shapely.

As he bent to kiss her she suddenly giggled, and rolled away from him,

slithering under the covers. He stood up and regarded her with amusement. This was going to be better than he had expected! Slowly he disrobed, and she lifted the sheets for him to slip in beside her, giving a tempting glimpse of her limbs as she did so.

Still in silence, he leaned over her to snuff the candle, but she caught his hand in hers.

'Do you wish to be in darkness?' she whispered softly.

Surprised, he looked down at her, and she grinned impishly.

'You have been complimenting me. May I not return the compliment? You are handsome, and good to look at. I would not wish to lose the pleasure of looking at you.'

Basely the thought flashed through his mind that she might simply find the attentions of a handsome man a welcome change, but he recalled that Dick Ashford was, in a different way, a goodlooking man. And he strongly suspected that Dick Ashford had been

in the same bed on the previous night.

Dismissing the thought, he left the candle to illuminate the scene, and made the most of his opportunities. He soon found that she was as expert as he in the art of love, and it was a long time before they lay quiet in one another's arms.

She lay still for a while, and then ran her fingers lightly over the long scar on his chest.

'Where did you gain this trophy?' she asked tenderly.

'What, that wound? Oh, 'twas some years since, we were defending some town, I forget which. We lost the town, I regret to say!'

He thought back to that occasion. He remembered it only too well, but could not tell her that it was a wound he had sustained when he had been covering the retreat of Charles Stuart from Worcester two years earlier. He thought back briefly to the rough bandaging he had been able to contrive before fleeing in the wake of the King, and the days he had spent in hiding at the house of a friend in Staffordshire, after an agonising ride when he had wondered whether he would be able to stay on his horse for long enough to reach the refuge. He had spent several days in delirium, and only the courage of his friend's wife had saved him. She had hidden him under her bed, and with the assistance of the village midwife, given a most convincing demonstration of a woman in labour when the troopers of Parliament had searched the house. Fortunately they had had sufficient warning of the approach of the troopers to smuggle her three month old baby out to one of the cottages nearby, where there were so many children that an extra one would not be noticed!

'Why then do you smile?' she asked. 'I would not have thought a wound and a lost battle cause for rejoicing.'

'I was remembering the lady who sheltered me and cared for me then,' he said truthfully, and was wickedly pleased to see a slight frown cross her face.

'Where were you fighting?'

'Mainly in Flanders. It was mostly seige warfare, which is mightily tedious. I had not the patience for it.'

'No, that I can well believe,' she murmured, and he mentally added a point to her score of tricks.

After a few moments of silence she spoke again.

'Why did you leave the army?'

'Partly that I was bored with it, for I have been in the army for ten years, since I was eighteen, and my father permitted me to join.'

'Did you not run away to join if you were so anxious?' she laughed mischievously.

'I thought of it, indeed, and considered myself most ill used to be forbidden. But with my father and elder brother Thomas in the army, my mother was frantic against my going, and I could not distress her by such an action.'

'So after achieving your wish, you became bored with army life? Is it so with you with everything you achieve?'

He kissed her. 'Indeed no. Are you afraid that I shall grow tired of your charms, my dear Cherry?'

'I did wonder,' she murmured. 'Mayhap I should have been more coy, pretended shyness?'

'You must not pretend. In some women it adds to their charms, but in others, like you, it detracts. Stay as you are.'

There was a pause, while they embraced.

'But the boredom was only part of the reason,' Miles went on. 'I did not wish to fight for the States against England, which might have been necessary. Also, I have just received a small inheritance, and have a mind to buy an estate and settle to the life of a country squire.'

'Methinks you would get bored with that even more swiftly than with soldiering,' she said seriously.

'Do you not like the country?'

'Not overmuch, I confess. I spent much of my childhood in Norfolk, and though my father was a merchant in Norwich, we had a house some distance away where I spent most of my time.'

'I would endeavour to spend a considerable time in London. Particularly — ' he paused, and she glanced up at him, laughter in her eyes.

'If you had something to do here,' she finished for him.

'That I did not get bored with,' he added softly, and proceeded to make love to her again, so that it was dawn for the second night running before Cherry eventually went to sleep.

3

Miles walked home to his lodgings in the early morning, confident that he had succeeded with Cherry, and that she would continue to welcome him to her house. With this advantage he would be in a good position to work for his master, Charles Stuart, and further his designs. He had no scruples about using Cherry in that way. She was obviously no innocent maiden, but neither, judging by the company that surrounded her, was she openly a whore. He was puzzled slightly, but soon concluded that she was simply a passionate woman who cleverly managed to keep her activities secret from those who would have disapproved of them.

Later in the day, he paid visits to several men who were known to be working more or less actively for the restoration of the King, and after presenting his credentials, discovered much of what was toward. This was not very encouraging. There were rumours of several plots, but from what Miles could learn they were neither well thought out nor efficiently organised. Since the Parliament had passed the Acts of Sale, forcing Royalists to lose their property, fewer of the King's nominal supporters had been willing to work openly for him, and the difficulties of clandestine plotting had made all but the most determined give up participation, if not hope. Combined with the forebearance shown to compounding Royalists, or to those returning from exile, the climate was not promising.

But not all was dark and gloomy. Miles heard of plans to seize the ports in the west, and the name of Robert Phelips, one of the men who had braved much to assist the King in his flight after Worcester, was mentioned frequently. Miles hoped that if there were any possibility of success here, the

King could return and attempt another battle, this time English led. He determined to visit Phelips in the west country.

Another name he heard mentioned frequently was that of Lord Belasyse, a member of the prominent Lord Fauconberg's family, Catholics, and wealthy northern landowners. Here was another possible contact who would be able to influence large groups of people. He would have to travel north too. His excuse of searching for a small estate would serve as reason for these journeys.

He was planning this as he emerged from a tavern in Fleet Street where he had been talking with one of his contacts, and trying to decide whether his regret at the need to leave London so soon after arriving there had too much to do with Cherry Weston, which would be dangerous to his mission, when he saw her.

At first he thought that he had been mistaken. It was the curve of the cheek and the pert little chin that had made him look twice at the woman who was hurrying past. Then he noted her clothes, almost ragged, and far from clean, and dismissed it as a chance resemblance. But, unconvinced, he turned round and stared after her. She was the same height, and had the same dark hair. Her gown was loose, and disguised her figure, but by now Miles was so uncertain that he began to walk unobtrusively after the woman.

Gradually he drew nearer, and watched her closely. She did not pause, but went purposefully onwards, until she reached Middle Temple Lane. As she turned into it she glanced back, and Miles was now certain that it was Cherry Weston he was following. She had not seen him, for he had been cautiously keeping in the shadows, and he decided to risk following her further. He was intrigued at this view of her in such clothes, for until this time she had always appeared in expensive, luxurious gowns. He determined to unravel this puzzle.

She reached the quarters where the students of the Inns had their lodgings, as well as other gentlemen who enjoyed such bachelor quarters. Looking cautiously round, she disappeared into one of the buildings, and Miles settled to wait, hidden from view in a doorway.

He pondered on this. Was she paying some clandestine visit to yet another lover? Why the clothes, which were too drab and poor to be used as a disguise, if that was her business. She looked like a servant, and a badly provided for one at that.

Miles did not however, have long to consider these ideas, for Cherry reappeared. She had scarcely been gone long enough for amorous dalliance, and the puzzle deepened, for if it were not this, what could it be?

She did not pause, but made her way back to Canning Street through the less frequented ways, and Miles followed as close as he dared. At length he saw her slip unobtrusively into the stable entrance of her own house, and he turned down a side road and made his way back to his own lodgings.

He had not solved the puzzle when he was next at Cherry's house, at a gathering similar to the one when he had first been welcomed there. As Cherry, elegantly gowned in a deep red satin greeted him, he eyed her speculatively. What was the answer?

Dick Ashford was already there, and greeted Miles pleasantly. Miles wondered what his relationship with Cherry was, and what his reaction would be when he discovered her liaison with himself. This would have to be treated with caution, for he did not wish to arouse jealousies that would endanger his work.

Faithful Denham was there too, and scarcely returned Miles' greeting, seeming to be preoccupied with his own gloomy thoughts. But several other guests who had been there on the earlier occasion recognised Miles, and he was drawn into their conversations.

Most of the talk was to do with the affairs of the country. Miles attached himself to a group surrounding an elderly plainly dressed man, who was being listened to with a great deal of respect as he talked, gesticulating as he made his points.

'You ask by what right we rule?'

'Aye,' replied a slim, young man. 'You are not elected members, you do not represent all the people.'

'To be elected after the fashion of older times does not make a Parliament more fitted to govern. None of our past Parliaments have proved worthy or capable of doing that well.'

'Mayhap not, but they were more readily accepted, as the people had placed them in their position.'

'We too, unworthy though we regard ourselves, have been placed there too. We did not select ourselves. We were nominated by men of good faith. Mayhap that is a superior method of choosing the Members than the old way.'

'How much say did Oliver have in the nominations?' asked a third man.

'What of that? He is the only man strong enough to bring the Army and the Parliament together for the good of the whole country,' The Member paused, looking round the group. 'You do not think we are doing this for our own aggrandisement, as so many of the Rump were? We do not seek spoils. We protested at our unworthiness, and only accepted the task laid upon us as a duty. God must be served in many ways, and some of us have been called upon to serve Him in this way, in bringing the country back to the path of righteousness, in showing the people how to be holy. That is our divinely appointed task, and we will not shirk it, whatever calumnies are directed at us.'

'I do not question your reasons, not yet your intentions,' the young man replied. 'I but wonder whether the people will be willing to be ruled by you. There are stirrings already, in the west in particular.'

'There are always those disaffected under any rule. We shall seek them out. We have good warnings of the evil plots that abound, and will pounce when the time is right.'

'I trust so.' Cherry had joined the group. 'Do not leave it too late, I beg of you, Mr. Carver. I shudder whenever I hear of such plots, and think myself like to be murdered one dark night. I am afraid to go abroad even in the daytime when these rumours are rife.'

'Do not be concerned, dear lady. We have the matter well in hand, and methinks in but a few days you will know more,' Mr. Carver reassured her.

'Is it possible that you will encourage more dissatisfaction by this?' the young man persisted. 'Already there are signs of restlessness, whispers of dictator-ships.'

'Fie, Mr. Taunton. We are no dictators. We do not wish to maintain our rule. We look upon the next fifteen months of our Parliament as a time of toil and worry, not a delight to us. Do you not realise that at the end of that time, we are to choose another Parliament? None of us serving today will be overready to serve again. We all have our own businesses to see to, and take on the present task out of our love of God, and our desire to make the country holy.'

The young man, Taunton, did not look entirely convinced, but he smiled and nodded.

'I am certain that you will perform your tasks admirably, Mr. Carver,' Cherry said, and smiled around the group. They nodded in agreement. 'As for me,' she went on, 'if I had any choice in the matter at all, I would be content for people like you and Mr. Denham and Mr. Ashford to continue ruling us. 'Tis only with strong men that I feel safe!'

'You are not safe from temptation, ever,' intoned Faithful, who had drifted across to the group. 'God seeks to entrap the unwary, those who do not watch their every action.'

'Then 'tis good that we will have rulers who will point the temptations out to us, Mr. Denham. Come,' Cherry took his arm and moved away with him, 'I want to introduce you to Mistress Browne. She needs advice, and asked me if I could suggest a godly man to help her.'

Miles, suppressing a desire to laugh, turned to the young man beside him.

'We have not been introduced. Miles Talbot, sir.'

'John Taunton. I have not seen you here before?'

'No, 'tis but my second visit. I am newly back in England. Think you these plots are more serious this time? None until now have seemed to be more than the wild ravings of madmen, who think that they can march on London with a few pikes, and have the citizens quaking with fear of them.'

Taunton laughed. 'Aye, that is all it has been till now, but this seems somewhat more. It centres on several ports in the west, and is widespread. That is what I mean when I say that there is dissatisfaction, but people like Carver are so convinced of their rightness that 'tis left to others to protect them and maintain them in their position.'

'Are you in the Army?' Miles asked.

'No. I am concerned with supplies to the Navy. That is how I come by my information.'

Dick Ashford joined them at that moment, and clapped Miles on the shoulder.

'Here, comrade, do not be drowned in serious talk! There is enough of that elsewhere without turning these evenings into minor Parliamentary meetings. Do you intend to go to Moorfields tomorrow? There is to be a display you must not miss. The Army has something special in mind for the drilling.'

' 'Tis worth seeing?' Miles asked.

'Aye,' Mr. Taunton told him, looking

more cheerful. 'They are most impressive to watch even on ordinary occasions, when they do but drill in their normal fashion, but I have seen marvellous displays of mock battles, and reconstructions of sieges. I shall most certainly be there. Will you join me?'

'I would be delighted.'

'Will you both dine with me beforehand, at the Mermaid in Cheap?' Dick asked, and so arrangements were made.

The rest of the evening passed very pleasantly. There was music for a while, and plentiful wine and delicious food. Miles was drawn into conversation with a group of merchants and their wives, and found himself being determinedly ogled by one of the younger wives, a girl of little more than twenty. She was, it transpired, married to an elderly man Miles had at first taken for her grandfather. She contrived to sit beside him in a narrow space, and pressed her leg against his more closely than the constricted space demanded. When he glanced at her, she was trying to appear unconcerned, but proved very ready to enter into conversation with him. Amused, he flirted mildly with her, and was not surprised when she mentioned casually that she lived in the next house to Cherry, and hoped that he would call on her some day.

'My husband is usually so busy, he cannot spend as much time with me as we both would wish,' she simpered and Miles looked at her in disbelief, causing her to blush furiously as she read the expression in his eyes. 'He encourages me to entertain my friends,' she continued hurriedly. 'Cherry Weston is always popping in and out, as I am with her. I do hope you will call in when you are near.'

'I will certainly avail myself of your invitation,' he murmured, wondering to himself whether he would, for she was too insipid for his taste and too eager to make him notice her. He found himself comparing her with Cherry, who did not need to do more than appear in a room for everyone to be aware of her. I will visit her if it proves necessary for my mission, he found himself mentally promising, then realised that he now had no such conditions in mind when he thought of visiting Cherry. He frowned. She was getting too great a hold on him, and that would be disastrous. He could not, in his way of life, afford to fall in love. So far the temptation had not come to him, he had been able to enjoy women casually, and leave them when the time came without regrets. He must be careful.

'What are you thinking?' his flirtatious neighbour asked playfully.

'I was wondering what your name was,' he said unblushingly, and she giggled in delight.

' 'Tis Anne Aston,' she told him.

'Anne,' he repeated softly, caressingly, and she looked down in confusion, and hurriedly began to talk of something else.

Soon, to Miles' secret relief Mr. Aston decided that it was time for him to go, and he carried away his pouting wife who cast an appealing glance back at Miles as they left. Several others followed his lead, and within half an hour most of the guests had departed.

The few that remained were the younger set, Dick and Mr. Taunton, Miles, two young married couples and, to Miles' surprise, Faithful Denham, who sat himself determinedly by the fire where, in spite of its being midsummer, a small fire of logs glowed.

Cherry sat beside Mr. Taunton and engaged him in conversation, but they were too far away for Miles to overhear what they were saying, though he could see that Taunton was flattered at the attention she was paying him. He glanced across at Dick, but he did not appear to be noticing, engrossed in conversation with one of the young husbands. Miles joined the other young guests, and they demanded that he tell them about Flanders, as they had discovered that he was recently there. He complied, and repeated his reasons for returning home. A heated discussion arose as to where he should look for a property, Oxfordshire and Kent being the favoured areas, but he laughingly said that he meant to travel a great deal before deciding.

Eventually, they broke up the party. Dick departed with one couple, and Taunton, reluctantly it seemed to Miles, prepared to accompany the others who were going in his direction.

'Mr. Denham comes your way too,' Cherry remarked casually. 'As for you, Mr. Talbot, you go quite the other way. You will have to take care, out alone at this time.'

Faithful seemed reluctant to go, but was cleverly managed by Cherry, who talked vivaciously as she unobtrusively moved with them to the front door. Faithful found himself walking away with the others, and Miles was alone with Cherry. She stood watching them until they turned the corner, and then stepped back into the house, making no attempt to wish him farewell, as he had made no attempt to remain outside.

'Would you care for a last glass of wine?' she asked, and laughed as he took her into his arms.

'Nectar is what I am going to have,' he told her, and led her into the bedroom, where, as before, the candle was already waiting.

They made love slowly, lingeringly, coming together with a fierce passion, and then lying contentedly together.

Cherry once more traced the line of the scar across his chest, and leant over him to kiss it.

'I feel safe with you,' she murmured. 'No talk of plots frightens me when you are here.'

'I do not think you need fear aught,' he said, wondering whether she really was afraid.

'Do you think 'tis all moonshine? Or are there really plotters working away against the government?'

'There are bound to be plots when many of the people resent the present rulers,' he said cautiously.

'That is what John Taunton says. He seems to know some details. It frightens me. Is he right?'

'I do not know what he does. Remember I have but recently returned here.'

She was winding one of his curls round her finger, and at this she smiled, and pulled it slightly.

' 'Twas my fortune that you did so while Robert was still in London,' she whispered, glancing through her lashes at him. 'What if we had never met? Who else might have introduced us? Have you other friends here, or are you completely alone?'

'I have a few acquaintances,' he said slowly. 'There are old friends I must look up. But I have been away so long, I fully expect that most of them will have forgotten me.'

'Then, though I am sorry if it makes you feel lonely, I am pleased if it means you will have more time for me.'

'I shall give you no peace,' he promised, and tried to kiss her. She responded passionately at first, and then moved away.

'Tell me more about yourself. I know so little, and it torments me. I do not even know where you live, so that if you desert me, I could not come in search of you!'

'What would you know of me? Is it not enough that I am here, that you are here, and we have found one another?'

'It may be sufficient for you, but not for me, I wish to be able to imagine at any time of the day what you are doing, who you are with.'

'Might you not be jealous?' he teased, and she laughed.

'If you mean poor Anne Aston, by no means! She considers herself mightily wicked to flirt with a man in public, but I suspect that if one tried to as much as kiss her in private, she would scream the house down.'

'You tempt me to assay it!'

'You have been warned! But I do not think you will. You are not the man to be attracted by her charms. No, I imagine you spending a deal of time talking politics with your friends in taverns, or riding, mayhap hunting or racing. Am I right?'

'You are always right,' he said evasively, and his slight suspicions hardened when she continued to ask questions.

'Do bring any friends you wish to invite to my gatherings. As Robert brought you. I welcome new faces.'

'I know that,' he told her, laughing, 'and 'tis a very good reason why I should not care to introduce a possible rival!'

'Miles!' she protested, laughing. 'Do you fear that I am weary of you? Already? You must think me most inconstant if you fear to lose me so soon. I shall expect you to bring your friends now merely to prove that you do not fear that!'

He laughed, and protested that he was far from thinking so, but he was beginning to wonder at her persistence in trying to discover his friends. He admired her technique, and was highly suspicious that he was far from the first man she had questioned in such a way. What exactly was she doing? Was she one of the spies Parliament employed to track down the people disaffected with their rule? It was unusual for one such to work from so open a connection with the Parliamentarians, but it was certain that the men responsible for intelligence would be expecting efforts to infiltrate such a group, as he was trying to do. Mayhap Cherry was one of the first lines of defence.

He did not have time to ponder this, for Cherry had begun to ask questions about his childhood home, and his family. Apart from concealing their exploits on the side of the Kings during the wars, he was able to tell her a great deal, amusing her with tales of his adventures as a boy. She responded with stories of her own girlhood, and they lay and talked for most of the night.

Cherry was equally puzzled. She had

an instinctive feeling that he was not the same as men like Dick Ashford, and was not in sympathy with her guests, but she could not analyse why. In some way she was afraid of him. It briefly crossed her mind to wonder if he was employed by Mr. Thurloe, who had six months before been put in charge of intelligence, and was spying on her. She well knew that under the influence of her wine and pleasant company her guests were more forthcoming than perhaps they should be. Were the authorities becoming anxious?

However, she dismissed such thoughts, and set herself to charm Miles, admitting to herself that for once it was exceptionally easy to forget everything, even Harry, who had been brought to mind so vividly when she first saw Miles. By this time she found no resemblance between the two men, Miles having driven all thoughts of Harry from her as she came to know him better.

4

Miles enjoyed an excellent dinner at the Mermaid tavern with Dick Ashford and John Taunton, before accompanying them to Moorfields to see the display by the Army. It was a most impressive reconstruction of the battle of Langport, and Miles, who remembered the time when he had witnessed the New Model Army in action on the field, had his awareness of their excellence renewed. He had not himself been at Langport, but had heard from a friend who had survived the battle of the incomparable valour of the Ironsides. Now the Army was bent on reminding the people of London of its reputation.

Afterwards, Dick took them off to his lodgings, where he eagerly discussed the tactics of the battle with Miles. John Taunton had laughingly excused himself on the plea that he knew nothing of the art of fighting, and amused himself reading some of the news sheets he found lying on a table.

'Why do you collect this stuff?' he asked later, when the two ex-soldiers had exhausted their comments, and they were all seated round the supper table.

'I find it useful, as a Member, to know the sort of things that are being cried against us.'

'Are there many such circulating?' Miles asked, picking one up and skimming through it.

'More than we care for, especially as they are all against the law. But 'tis plaguey difficult to discover those responsible. We do our best to track them down, but unless we receive information, we can rarely catch the miscreants.'

'Think you 'tis a sign of discontent, or merely a few troublemakers?' Miles queried.

Dick shrugged. 'There are always those discontented. In the present circumstances, with so many still pining for the return of those miserable Stuarts, God knows why, this stuff is easy to sell, and failing buyers to give away.'

'We shall not be rid of it until there is a free Parliament,' Taunton declared.

Dick laughed. 'Aye, you keep repeating that. It may be what people want, but is it what is best for them?'

'That scarce matters. If they have what they want, they will cease some of their grumblings.'

'Some, never will they cease all.'

'What happens to the men who circulate these?' Miles asked.

'Sometimes a fine. We are short of money, you understand?' Dick laughed. 'Besides, why should we burden the prisons with them? We need the room there for more dangerous rebels. Those who merely shout rarely take action, and 'tis they we are most concerned with.'

'Have there been many plots?'

'More than is generally thought. But

we have an excellent system of gathering information. Little passes but that we get to hear of it. Charles Stuart is not going to slip back onto the throne through want of vigilance on our part.'

'There seems to be little likelihood of his return,' Miles suggested.

'None whatsoever. The people of England will not suffer that oppression again.'

Nothing more was said about plots or plotters, and Miles soon took his leave. It was on the following day that he heard the first rumours of arrests. He spent a great deal of time at various taverns, trying to obtain news, but it was not until he was at Cherry's that evening that he heard certain news.

Faithful Denham was holding forth when he arrived, and Miles soon discovered that there had been a wave of arrests in the western counties.

'Their wickednesses have been discovered, they shall be punished,' Faithful was declaring. 'Arch traitors, all of them. The rot was widespread, but it has been stopped, and by example shall others be made aware of the punishments that await the ungodly.'

Miles glanced around. A few of the faces showed a little amusement at Faithful's vehemence, but the majority of the listeners were drinking it in, nodding in agreement at what he was saying. Miles wondered anxiously how much of the plotting he had himself heard of from Royalist sources had indeed been uncovered.

'How many have been arrested, then?' he asked the man next to him.

' 'Tis rumoured hundreds,' the man replied excitedly. 'From Portsmouth to Plymouth the traitors have been taken I hear.'

Miles wondered if this was another exaggeration, for if the man were right in his estimate, there would be few plotters left in the west country.

'They are bringing some of the ringleaders to London, and they will be put in the Tower,' his informant went on. 'I trust that a good example be made of them, to warn others that might be tempted to do likewise that we will not suffer it.'

The mood that night was one of jubilation, and Miles was hard put to it to join the general rejoicings. But he succeeded in disguising his apprehension, and seemed as pleased as the rest that the government was taking such good care to ensure that those that disagreed with it were silenced.

Cherry made an excuse to come across to Miles quite soon in the evening. She leant close to him as he sat on a chair, and after a few general remarks, whispered quietly.

'You will stay later?'

Intoxicated by the subtle perfume that she used, and her nearness, and hot with desire for her, he was tempted to throw caution to the winds and accept the invitation, but he had resolved to be wary of her. He was suspicious of her questions, that seemed so innocent, but were so cleverly designed to wheedle information out of the unwary. He was not afraid of giving himself away, for he was too old a hand at the game, but he was afraid of her effect on him, and the feelings she aroused in him that no other woman had yet succeeded in tapping. He was on the verge of falling in love, and he shuddered to think of the complications that could bring to his mission, especially as she was on the other side in the battle of wits.

He knew that he was not strong enough to avoid her completely, but had resolved that he must not make a habit of visiting her alone. He still needed to mix with her friends, but coolly decided that if she herself had any information of value to him, she would be more likely to divulge it unknowingly if he could bemuse her by keeping her passion for him, which he knew to be as great as his for her, at fever heat.

So he sighed regretfully, and shook his head.

'I have to start early in the morning,' he said quietly. 'I am going to visit several properties, and take a look at different parts of the country. You know I would not readily forego the pleasure of a night with you, but I have already spent longer here than I intended. You have entrapped me. I should have been away from London some days since.'

Cherry smiled, trying not to let him guess that she was herself relieved. She too was harbouring suspicions of this handsome man who had suddenly burst into her life, and was virtually unaccounted for. She had not intended to issue the invitation when she had come across to speak with him, but standing beside him, had suddenly heard herself doing so. She inwardly chided herself that she was losing her hold on herself, that she did not beg men for favours.

'Then I wish you a pleasant journey, and hope that you will come and see me when you return,' she said, trying to indicate that she was indifferent whether he did so or not, but failing, as they both knew full well.

'Indeed I will,' he said looking deep into her eyes, so that she looked away with difficulty, suddenly remembering her other guests.

Miles did not speak with her again until he rose to go, fairly early in the evening, when several other guests were still there.

Cherry had spent the last ten minutes deep in conversation with John Taunton, and the young man was visibly flattered. Miles wondered cynically if he was to be substituted that night, and suppressed a pang of jealousy as she smiled intimately at Taunton before crossing to bid the departing guests farewell.

'My thanks for your hospitality,' Miles said, taking her hand and holding it firmly in his.

'I trust you will partake of more when you return, Mr. Talbot,' she returned, and without enquiring when that was likely to be, dismissed him and turned to another. Miles could not but admire her self control, and he took himself off with haste, walking rapidly back to his lodgings where he packed his saddlebags ready for the early departure he had planned.

Several hours later he ruefully admitted to himself that he might as well have stayed with Cherry if all he had been concerned at was a full night's sleep. For the first time in his life, experienced soldier as he was, he was unable to sleep when he wished. Images of Cherry kept dancing before his eyes, and he writhed as he imagined her sporting with John Taunton, or Dick Ashford, or another of her no doubt many lovers.

Heavy eyed and in a black mood, he rose at dawn, and was soon riding out on the Bath road.

After some hours of hard riding, he was able to bring his thoughts to the ruin of the plots in the west. He planned to visit Robert Peyton, who, though not actively involved in the plotting himself, knew a great deal of what went on, and sometimes acted as messenger or agent for the Royalists, who all knew that he could be trusted.

When he reached Robert's house he was made welcome by Robert and his pretty wife, Jane, but there was an air of strain, and as soon as they were alone without the servants, they began to talk. Robert told of the many arrests that had been made.

'They have quietly been taking people for some days past,' he explained. 'Some managed to escape once they realised that all was discovered, but the vast majority of the leaders have been imprisoned. Phelips is amonst them. It means that we must start afresh here in the west.'

'You will need new leaders. How are they to be found?' Miles asked.

'There are many men willing to risk all for the cause,' Robert said thoughtfully, 'but there are few of sufficient stature to be recognised as leaders, and so to influence others. Those that were not involved in this plot have been very remote of late. Mayhap they have forsaken us, mayhap they are avoiding suspicion, and would join in again later.'

'We must hope that the latter is the situation. I will visit them, and endeavour to spur them to action. I have many names, but hope that you can furnish me with others.'

'Indeed yes. When they see that you come from the King himself, they will be more ready to join you,' Jane said encouragingly.

'Unless this latest discovery has frightened them again,' Robert said.

'I hope 'tis simply that they need guidance on what to do. The sort of risings that have been planned are of little value unless they are coordinated, and there is a general move throughout the country. That is partly what I hope to encourage, but there must be leaders that are widely respected. If I can sound some of these men, and discover which of them are ready, and how far they will commit themselves, that will be a basis on which to work.'

So it was arranged. Miles spent the last two weeks of August riding around the counties of Devon and Somerset, and made one journey into Cornwall. He then contacted people in Wiltshire, and was ready, early in September, to bid the Peytons farewell, being reasonably pleased with the encouragement he had received. The people only needed leadership, and the prospect of a reasonable chance of success, and they would move. It remained to provide that leadership.

Armed with the names of several prominent supporters in the counties to the north, Miles set off once more. He travelled slowly through Gloucestershire and the midland counties, and eventually found a man likely to command sufficient support to be a credible leader. This was Lord Belasyse, the younger son of Lord Fauconberg.

Miles spent a considerable time with Lord Belasyse and his friends, discussing the possibilities, and making known to them the King's views. They seemed ready to make some move, and he left with their promise to send one of their number to consult with him in London later in the year.

On leaving the north, Miles made his way back towards London through the eastern counties, which had been fiercely Parliamentarian during the wars, but where there were many fervent Royalists. He met several of these in Norfolk, and found them equally ready to become involved in plotting. After many consultations it was agreed that they also would send a representative, and after Miles had had time to report on the prospect to the King, firm plans could be made.

Before he left Norfolk to return to London, Miles was taken one night to visit a relative of Sir Edward Villiers, another man he had marked as a possible leader.

This was a Sir Henry Villiers, another of the vast clan of relatives of the Duke of Buckingham. Miles found a pleasant man a few years younger than himself, but already the father of a growing family. Lady Villiers, heavily pregnant, made him welcome but soon disappeared, leaving Miles and Sir Henry alone with Sir Edward who explained what they wanted.

'Henry, you have been acting for some time as a channel for information between the King and the Royalists at home. Would it be possible to add the collection of information about plots, so that you could inform the rest of us what is going on?'

'We envisage a central point where all the information can be gathered, from many sources,' Miles said. 'In the organisation we plan, 'tis essential that all risings or plots shall be centrally directed, so that they have the most possible value to us. We hope that all the plotters will come to trust us with their plans, and take our advice.'

Sir Henry laughed. 'Do not take it amiss if I say that you will be fortunate to have a quarter of them do so.'

Miles grinned back at him. 'I do realise the magnitude of the task, but if only we can start with the right people at the head, there is hope that in time most of the Royalists will come to work together. They will see that 'tis the best way.'

'But Jermyn, and Hyde, and Rupert's Swordsmen do not work together, if all we hear is true.'

'They propose different solutions to the problem, aye,' Miles rejoined. 'The King does not favour one more than another, and he is ready to consider any way that holds hope of success. He wishes to be guided by the people in England too, for they know more of the temper of the country than he can in exile.'

'What would you have me do?'

'I understand that you live in London normally?'

'Aye. As a younger son with little prospects, I had to make my own way in the world, and so I became a lawyer. It serves as a cover for my activities. I can see many people, and if I visit odd places, 'tis to do with my work.'

'Then you could be available for people to give you information, and pass it on to us?'

'That should present no difficulties. I do not imagine there will be hundreds of plotters crowding my lodgings?'

'Unfortunately not,' Miles laughed. 'Thank you for your help. When do you return to London?'

'After my wife is safely delivered, which should be during the next two weeks. I will be in London at the very latest by mid November.'

'Where will I find you?'

Sir Henry gave him an address in Clifford's Inn, and suggested that Miles called at the beginning of the month, and if he were still out of London, leave the address of his own lodging.

'You may find it expedient to move around,' he advised. 'Then one's neighbours do not become too familiar with one's habits, and suspicious of visitors.'

'I will be in touch,' Miles agreed.

'How is Emma this time, Henry?' Sir Edward asked, as they drank the wine and chatted over other things.

'She is well. 'Twas a great disappointment to us both last year when we lost the child she was carrying, but all has gone well this time, and we are hoping for another girl.'

'So that you will have three of each? 'Tis a goodly family in just seven years, is it not, Mr. Talbot?'

'Indeed yes, you must be proud of them,' Miles responded, warming to the other's animation and enthusiasm when he talked of his family. He wondered that a man with so much to risk should be willing to work for the King, but knew that many others were doing the same, for a cause they believed in as firmly as they did in God.

Miles had a few more visits to make in Norfolk and then he moved on to Essex. By the time he returned to London he was satisfied that he had done all he could to set in motion the beginnings of a proper organisation to work for the King's restoration.

He planned to spend the time before he saw Sir Henry again in making contact with the known Royalists in London, and apprising them of the new arrangements. He must send a report of his activities to the King, but at the present stage in the arrangements it was essential for him to be in London. He would await the King's reply, and in the meantime work on the plans. Later, if it were necessary, he could go himself to see the King after the meeting he had arranged with the various representatives.

It was early in November when he reached London, having been absent for well over two months. As he rode into the City, he felt the rising excitement at the thought of seeing Cherry again. During his long absence, the thought of her had tormented him, and his longing for her had not abated. He had tried to forget her with the very willing and pretty landlady at one of the inns he had stayed in, but after the first slaking of his need, had had to confess to himself that there was no delight in making love with anyone but Cherry. After that time he had been impervious to the many lures that had been cast after him, contenting himself with making sure that he enslaved the wives, sisters, and daughters of the conspirators, without giving their menfolk cause to object to him. He judged, cynically, that if he implied promises and expressed admiration, the women would encourage their men to do what he asked in the way of supporting the King. So far he was willing to go, but he doubted his ability to pretend to greater passion with any degree of conviction, should the need arise in the future. He cursed the effect Cherry had had on him in destroying this ability, which had been one of his greatest assets in the past.

5

Returning to his old lodgings, Miles sent a boy with a note to Cherry, and then sat before the fire drinking wine, and allowing his thoughts to dwell on her. When the boy returned, he took the note impatiently, having rewarded the lad. He almost pushed him out of the room, and then opened the screw of paper.

It was brief, but he smiled in satisfaction. Cherry wrote that she happened to be free that evening, and suggested that he came for supper. Interpreting this to mean that they would be alone, his first thoughts were thankfulness that he would not have to endure a whole evening of polite conversation with numerous other guests before he could take her in his arms. Then he wondered whether he was simply fortunate to find her disengaged, or whether she had put off other arrangements for his benefit.

It was almost time to go, and he changed into a wine coloured coat and breeches, which had ample lace decoration, silver buttons, and heavy embroidery. He called for a link boy, and set out, fuming with impatience at the boy's leisurely progress.

At last he arrived, and was admitted by one of Cherry's menservants who took him immediately to the small boudoir next to her bedroom.

She was waiting for him, dressed in a loose gown of pale green satin. When the servant announced him, she rose from the chair, and stood gripping the arms of it tightly while he made his bow. The servant withdrew, and he held out his arms, moving across the room towards her. With a low cry, she let go of the chair, and came to him. They kissed hungrily, and it was several minutes before either of them spoke.

'How I have missed you!' Miles said at length, holding her close and looking searchingly into her face as if to discover changes in it.

'I too.' She laughed a little unsteadily. 'I began to wonder if you would ever return. I thought mayhap you had found your estate, and decided to remain on it.'

'I returned as soon as 'twas possible,' he told her. 'I have been in London little more than an hour.'

'You have ridden far? You must be weary. Forgive me, I am keeping you standing!' She laughed and moved to one of the chairs, waving him to another. 'Would you prefer to eat now, or have some wine?'

He remained standing, smiling down at her.

'I am hungry for neither food nor drink. I was hoping that you would offer me what I do hunger for. I am weary of standing looking at you, and could think of better ways!'

'You are forthright, sir!' she chided mockingly, but rose willingly enough when he took her hand, and led her into the bedroom.

Their reunion was rapturous, for Cherry had been as impatient as Miles for his return, but had had the burden of not knowing when or even whether he would come. She had thought much about him during his absence, puzzling over what little she knew, suspicious of him. While he seemed ready to talk, and had told her much about himself, she admitted that her questions had been of little use. He had adroitly avoided imparting the information she sought, and though it had been done cleverly enough, it was clear to her that he was on his guard. Why? Who and what was he? Was he using her, trying to obtain information from her or from her guests? And if so, for what purpose?

And so she had determined to be wary of him, and to restrict their meetings, though she knew herself well enough to realise that she would find it difficult to refuse him. She had never felt like this before for any man, not even for Harry, her first love, whose memory had stayed fresh in her thoughts long after she had ceased to love him.

But when she had received his note, simply saying that he had returned and hoped to see her soon, she had dismissed all thoughts of caution in her fierce longing to be once more in his strong arms. She had thanked her good fortune that she had planned a quiet evening visiting a young married couple who lived nearby, and had without hesitation sent a note excusing herself, explaining that she had a slight fever. She smiled wryly to herself as she wrote the word 'slight', thinking that it poorly described her state.

After their first storm of passion was spent, they lay and talked, telling of what had happened during their separation. Miles described some of the houses he had visited, implying that they were possible purchases, and explained his extended absence by saying that he had felt it incumbent on him to visit the friends he had in the areas he had passed through. Cherry replied with some news about events in London, but little of moment had occurred.

'Now,' she said, after a while. 'Will you partake of the supper that is awaiting you? I arranged that it should be cold, and that we could serve ourselves.'

He smiled in appreciation.

'You anticipated some delay?' he asked softly.

'I did not know what to expect. Mayhap you would be late in coming,' she replied demurely, and had to protest when he began to kiss her again.

Eventually they slipped on loose robes, Cherry offering Miles one from the press, and looking mischievously at him as she waited for him to comment on her possession of such a garment large enough for him. He decided to tantalise her by ignoring it, and accepted without comment. They moved into the dining parlour, and sat at the table which had been drawn close to a brightly burning fire.

'Now bring me up to date with all that has been going on,' he asked, as they helped themselves to the food laid ready. 'I feel such a country bumpkin, away from affairs. Besides, I have been wondering whether I might not hope to be elected for Parliament when this present one comes to the end of its term. Then I would have ample reason for visiting London.'

He smiled at her, and she laughed. 'Methinks you do not need pretences for what you wish to do, Miles.'

'No, but 'tis convenient to have them. What has the Parliament been doing?'

'They have done as Faithful Denham promised, in hope of making the people holy. They have passed many laws forbidding such entertainments as bull baiting, and closed down cockpits, and theatres. 'Tis forbidden to dance round the maypole, and many other similar things. The punishments for doing so are severe.'

'Do you not think this is unwise of

them?' he asked slowly. 'They are harmless amusements, and the people will resent being made holy against their will!'

She looked at him quickly, then glanced down, her suspicions reawakened. She had forgotten this while they were making love. Was he trying to trap her into criticism of these new laws?

'They can do nought about it if they do,' she temporised. 'Those who break the law are usually fined, for there is much need of money, and many people in the prisons.'

'Aye. What of all the people arrested after their plotting was discovered? I heard little more about them.'

'Some have been released. I think the fright is like to prevent their joining in more conspiracies. The leaders are still held, apart from a few who escaped.'

'Are the gaols not secure, then?' he asked.

'I do not know how 'tis contrived. I hear that much money is used for bribes, and there are secret supporters of Charles Stuart amongst the warders. 'Tis to be expected in a divided nation.'

'How divided do you think the people are?'

'How can I tell? There are always the discontented, even when we have a Parliament that works hard as this one does to right the evils. Though even — ' she stopped, and looked confused.

'What would you say? Is there trouble?'

'No, I do not think so, yet.'

'What has happened that could cause trouble?'

'Well,' she considered her words carefully, ''tis felt by some people that Parliament is trying to do too much. Some of them have been critical of the General, and the Army does not like this. Then Parliament tried to claim the right to make appointments in the Army.'

'That would indeed antagonise the Army,' Miles said thoughtfully. He had not heard of this during his travels, and wondered what repercussions there might be if there was dissention between Parliament and the Army.

'What does Dick Ashford think of it?' he asked suddenly, watching her closely to see how she reacted at his mentioning that name, but she merely shrugged.

'He is a Member, and has said nought to make me think he does not agree with all that goes on.'

'But as a soldier . . . Besides, he did not seem the sort of man to wish to ban all amusements.'

'He has said nought.'

'And you, Cherry? Do you find these new laws irksome? I have often regretted that dancing is frowned upon, for I would dearly love to dance with you.'

A gleam came into her eyes, and was swiftly suppressed, but not before Miles had seen it.

'You are tempting me to turn traitor to my friends and to Parliament?' she asked, deciding to attack.

'What matters it between ourselves? Are we not already breaking the laws and liable for severe punishments, should my visits to you be discovered?'

'Do you wish me to turn you out, and refuse to see you again?' she asked, leaning towards him so that her gown fell partly open and he caught a glimpse of her breasts. 'Or will you risk three months in gaol, with no bail allowed?'

'Is that the penalty? 'Tis a small price to pay for a night with you, apart from the inability of repeating the offence! Would you come to gaol with me, Cherry? Would you help to pass the time?'

'I would be in a different gaol, methinks,' she laughed at him, and, relieved that the conversation had turned from the dangerous channels where she had to take such care over what she said, she made but token resistance when he suggested that they retire again to bed.

When Miles had finally dragged himself away, Cherry was no nearer solving her problem as to his motives in questioning her. She was well aware that there were many spies about whose task was to incriminate anyone who seemed to be against the rulers of the day. The very fact that she entertained Miles was sufficient to condemn her in many eyes, yet she had taken that risk, feeling that Miles was himself at a disadvantage if he attempted to use that against her. But he could well be laying a trap for her, hoping to discover resentments against the government, and then she would either be punished, or forced to work against her friends, trying to obtain evidence of disaffection amongst them. With the wide circle of acquaintances she had, and the vast amount of entertaining she did, she was in an excellent position to perform such tasks.

With immense difficulty she resolved that she must be alone with Miles as little as possible. During the next few months, difficult though she found it sometimes, she kept to that resolution for most of the time. To her relief, yet at the same time perverse regret, he did not press her for meetings. He came regularly to her house for the social gatherings, and sometimes she found herself, almost against her will, asking him to remain. He never refused, but he did not suggest staying of his own accord. She was sufficiently in control of herself not to arrange any more intimate suppers, but greatly missed them. She could not know that Miles was conscious of renewed suspicions of her, and fears that he might betray something of his missions if he became too accustomed to talking with her. He knew how fatally easy it was to let some word slip, that would give a great deal away to someone knowing what to look for.

In any event, Miles was busy during that November and December, and in the New Year had to undertake several journeys to different parts of England, and also to see the King.

Shortly after his return to London he was contacted by another agent who had just come to England. This was

Major Nicholas Armorer, who was also entrusted with the task of seeking out Royalist supporters and encouraging a movement for the restoration of the King.

They met in a tavern, and after drinking and talking together of innocuous matters, left to walk to Miles' lodgings. Here they could be private.

'What success have you had?' Nick asked, and Miles gave him details, and explained the arrangements that had so far been made.

'I hope that all the men I asked to come will be in London soon. There must be a meeting, and as you are so recently come over from the King, you had best be there if possible. They will be encouraged at hearing from you.'

'I have work to do that will keep me in London for some time. I will attend your meeting when 'tis fixed. You are satisfied with the men chosen?'

'They are as good as can be brought in. I contacted several on the list the King gave me who were unable or unwilling to offer more than good wishes, and mayhap some support if we organise an invasion, or start a rebellion against Parliament. Then I sounded several more who were recommended to me. The group of those prepared to put themselves in danger is small, and of those only a few have sufficient standing to be accepted as leaders by the rest. We must have prominent men, or the hope of a central direction to our plans will crumple, as each local plotter thinks he has the right to try his own ideas, and refuses to be guided or warned.'

'These men are important, and have good connections,' Armorer said, considering the list.

'But none of them are of the first rank. Oh, yes, they have birth, most of them, but they are all younger sons, and in most of the families there are those who are on the other side.'

''Tis hard to expect the heads of families to risk all by open rebellion.'

'True,' Miles agreed. 'I am myself a

younger son. But it makes the task so much more difficult.'

'They might be so sufficiently influential. But they are not our only hope. The King has many other schemes, even if some of them are as mad as Wogan's!'

'Wogan?' queried Miles. 'Do you mean that crazy Irishman? A Colonel, wasn't he?'

'Aye. First in the New Model, and he changed sides at Langdale, and brought his troop with him. Edward Wogan.'

'What has he been up to?'

'He has persuaded the King to allow him to try and recruit an army here.'

''Sdeath! He must be mad. If any army is to be formed, the only possibility is gradual recruitment under known and trusted leaders who lived in England, not foreign adventurers.'

'I agree, but 'tis a chance, and even if he fails, which is almost certain, 'twill give us an indication of how strong support for an armed rising is.'

'Is the King so desperate as to take

any such slight chance?'

'No, I do not think that is the case. Rather, would he seek to encourage all and every attempt, however wild. He would prefer his supporters to be willing to work together, but as they will not, being impatient like Wogan, he will not say them nay for fear of losing their support entirely. As with us, he prefers a central group to organise, but will not refuse other help. Indeed, there are times when he can scarce prevent these measures, even if he wants to.'

'Well, I wish Wogan good fortune, but have little hope for him. I judge that there is much discontent, and this will make it easier for us to involve people.'

'Have you heard aught of what goes on in Parliament?' Armorer asked.

'Aye. It seems that Barebones and his fellows become too presumptuous. They are demanding changes in the Army, and claiming the right to make appointments. That does not please Cromwell or the Army.'

'What is he like to do?'

'He set up this Parliament for fifteen months, yet it has had but four. If it tries his patience too greatly, he might do away with it. Also, the attempts at regulating the pleasures of the people are not popular. Englishmen are restive under Puritan rule, when their traditional sports are banned. There seems to be increasing avoidance of the law. Even the supporters of Parliament are somewhat uneasy at these developments, methinks.'

'There is hope there also, then, if more people become discontented.'

'Aye, but 'twill be a slow movement, unless some great event causes sudden change.'

'You are impatient?'

'Aye, who is not? We see so little of our work come to fruition, and must constantly start afresh as one promising avenue after another is closed to us.'

'There is a way through, never fear.'

'Oh, I do not despair. 'Tis merely that sometimes I would rather be out in the open fighting, as with Wogan, than burrowing secretly like a mole.'

Armorer smiled, for he knew Miles was one of the most devoted and clever agents Charles Stuart had working for him. He was not surprised that such thoughts should bother him, for they were familiar to everyone who had had to work in secret.

'I will contact you again if there is aught fresh you should know about, but the less we are seen together the better, methinks. I will leave regular reports with Sir Henry. Then we will meet when the people you have gathered come to London.'

On these arrangements, Miles bade Armorer farewell, and they both attended to their own business for the next few days.

Miles went once or twice to the address given by Sir Henry Villiers in Clifford's Inn, but it was yet early November, and the man had not yet returned from Norfolk. It was almost the middle of the month before Miles found him there.

'Welcome, Mr. Talbot,' Sir Henry said jovially when Miles was announced.

'My thanks, Sir Henry. You are in London in good time.'

'Aye, to be sure. My wife was prompt in presenting me with the child.'

'They are both well, I trust?' Miles enquired politely.

'Indeed so. Emma seems to thrive on childbearing, not puling and sickly like some women. And the girl, for 'twas a girl as we hoped, is big and strong.'

'You must be very proud of them both.'

'Indeed yes. Emma is a good wife, she does her duty uncomplainingly, and her dowry was a good one, it enabled me to become independent. I do not need to earn my living, hence I have time to help with your business.'

They began to discuss details of this, and Miles told Sir Henry what had been happening in London, and what new people he could expect to be visiting him with information or messages. He promised to bring Armorer soon, and Sir Henry added some comments of his own as to how the people were reacting to the decrees of Parliament.

'There is too much discontent for Cromwell to allow these Saints too great freedom. I believe there are those who urge him to take the government entirely into his own hands. They fear the Puritans, and he fears to hold proper elections for fear of Royalist success. If even his own puppets, as those 'Nominated' men are, will not do as he wishes, he must assume power.'

'That might be a setback to us, if he provides security for the people, and a liberal rule.'

'Aye, 'tis possible, for he is no hidebound Puritan of the same stamp as Barebones. Praise-God would call all pleasure sin, but Oliver relishes music and singing, and fine clothes. He would not seek to ban all that.'

'We must be prepared for some

changes soon. I trust we can counter them.'

He took his leave, and spent the next few days visiting Royalists in and near London. Then the meeting he had spent so much time contriving took place, and the men who had been chosen as leaders met together.

There were, besides Lord Belasyse and Sir Edward Villiers, Lord Loughborough, Colonel John Russell, Sir William Compton, and Sir Richard Willys. All, apart from the latter, were substantial property owners, but all were younger sons, so that it was only their own property they risked, not that of the rest of their family, if they should be taken and the land sequestrated. They were all influential in their own counties, and could depend on considerable support from friends and relatives. They had wide contacts, and Lord Belasyse, as a Catholic, was able to influence the people who had most experience of plotting and conspiracy in the penal times, but who, until now, had taken little part in plots for the restoration of the King.

The meeting was successful in that they agreed to form such a central organising and controlling body as the King wished. They accepted the King's commissions, and made plans for the future, organising the work each of them was to do, and arranging for contacts with Miles and Armorer.

Miles came away from it slightly disturbed, however. He could not set a reason for his vague unease about the Sealed Knot, as the organisation was to be known, unless it was the air of caution that had characterised everyone at the meeting. He chided himself for his mood of despondency, reasoning that it had been a first meeting, and time was needed to accustom them to working together in such a conspiracy. But this explanation did not satisfy him, and he determined that he would not omit to follow any other promising avenues.

6

It was shortly after the meeting of the Sealed Knot that Miles was visiting a Royalist near Barnet, when he met Colonel Wogan who was busy recruiting in the same area, and was dining at the same house.

Edward Wogan was a lively, audacious man, with plenty of Irish charm, and he had met Miles several times before, at the Court of the exiled Charles.

'Well met, Talbot!' he cried as Miles entered the room where Wogan was sitting with a couple of other men.

After the introductions, the talk was all of Wogan's plans and he was full of enthusiasm, though did not seem to be concerned that until now he had recruited but a dozen men.

'Will you not join us?' he asked Miles, and began to outline his plans.

'If I do not raise a large enough troop to be useful here, I shall march for Scotland, and make an attempt to win over the commanders there. 'Tis the only force we might expect help from that does not need to cross the sea to come to our aid. Come with us! You are an experienced officer, we need such men as you.'

For a long minute Miles was tempted. He had not supped with Cherry alone since that first night, and had managed to avoid staying behind after most of the social evenings he had spent at her house. She seemed to be avoiding him, too, and he jealously noted that John Taunton seemed to be in favour. But his longing for her was unabated, and it was only by forcing himself to concentrate fully on his work that he could push the image of her to the back of his mind. It was never entirely obliterated. Miles knew that Wogan's plan was almost certainly doomed to failure, and he was tempted to throw in his lot with the brave few, and die gloriously. He could see no future with Cherry, and no possibility of forgetting her. This might be the easiest way.

But these thoughts were only momentary. He was a soldier, under orders, if rather peculiar ones, and he served Charles Stuart. He could not throw up his own mission to seek oblivion in such a wild escapade. Reluctantly, he shook his head, and explained to Wogan that he had his own work to do.

'I wish you good fortune, however. You will inspire many, if not to follow your example, with hope that the cause is still alive, and this we must do. Once the mass of the people are prepared to accept the Commonwealth, we will have lost our chance to come back.'

'I understand your reasons, my friend, but think you are over cautious. These plots of yours are but pebbles on a beach. They are like to have no importance.'

'But we drop our pebbles into a pool,

and the ripples spread,' Miles laughed.

They parted with some regret on both sides, and Miles returned to London, where events were moving swiftly. One night at Cherry's he heard talk of the great discontent amongst the Members of Parliament.

'This man,' Faithful Denham was declaiming, 'Cromwell, is but a vulgar Army Officer. What right has he to dictate to us, the rulers of the country, those who would save its people from sin?'

'He did put you in that position in the first place,' John Taunton said mildly.

'He needed our help. He cannot do without our experience, yet he tries to prevent us from doing our duty. He will find that the people will not suffer that. They look to us to guide them to protect them from tyranny. This man is too puffed up in his own pride, he will not accept just rebukes, and honest guidance from us. He considers that he knows best all the time.'

'Mayhap he does, when it comes to making appointments within the Army,' Dick Ashford said. 'We were wrong, and I said so at the time, to try to insist that we made them. What do most of the Members know of Army matters?'

'You would say that,' Faithful spat furiously at Dick. 'You ought to be in the Army, not in Parliament, as you favour all they do so greatly. But how can men such as you know what is best? You are one of the ungodly, and unfitted to lead the people! If men knew as much about you as I do, they would whip you out of the City! If not worse!'

'What the devil do you mean?' Dick asked, angry and red faced.

'You know full well what I mean, you whoring bastard!' Faithful retorted, and would have said more had Cherry not intervened.

'Dick, Faithful! I beg of you, do not turn my parlour into a tavern, where brawls are common! Come, my friends,' she took Faithful's arm, and drew him to one side, 'do not offend me! I can well believe you have such disagreements amongst yourselves, but please, forget them for tonight. I have Madame Doria here especially to sing to us, and she is ready to entertain us now.'

Smiling, she made Faithful sit beside her on a settle, and though reluctant, he obeyed her wishes and relapsed into morose silence, while the lady Cherry had mentioned, unconcerned by the scene, sang several songs accompanying herself on a lute.

Afterwards, Cherry paid lavish attentions to Faithful, and Dick and John gathered with Miles. The talk at first was carefully free of references to Parliament or its doings, but Dick's resentment was great, and he began to complain about some of his fellows, who, he claimed, did not value what Cromwell was doing for the country.

'He has brought peace at home, and after a decade of war that is not to be scoffed at. Some of these fools would stir up trouble again by their intolerance, and their arrogance.'

''Tis strange that they desire to usurp the proper functions of the Army leaders,' Miles commented.

'Some of them would control our very thoughts as well as all our actions,' John said bitterly.

'Do many in Parliament feel as you do?' Miles asked sympathetically.

'A goodly number.' Dick was drinking heavily and speaking more openly than ever before in Miles' company. 'But the time is coming when we will have to show them that theirs is not the way free born Englishmen wish to be ruled. Rather a King again than that!'

Miles raised his eyebrows. 'What say you? Is there such feeling? How does it happen?'

'Oh, we do not mean to bring back Charles Stuart! That was not what I meant,' Dick went on. 'But there are times when a country can only be ruled by a strong man, who can depend on such support as is necessary. None of us desire the Stuarts, or any other family to be set over us, but a King by selection, as in the old days, one whom, because he had been chosen by the people, could have their support.'

'Do many think as you do? I confess 'tis a novel idea to me.'

'Many men will be thinking it soon,' John said confidently, but Dick then contrived to change the subject, either, Miles thought ruefully, because he suspected Miles as a stranger, or because he thought such claims were unimportant.

Miles did not long regret hearing no more about the possible selection of a King, which he interpreted to mean that Cromwell was considering some move against the Parliament, an important piece of information. Dick had other grievances, and proceeded to give details.

'We are being openly reviled in the City and elsewhere because of the frequent days of Public Humiliation. Merchants do not like to have to shut their booths so often, and the apprentices are openly playing the banned games. It makes people look back to times when they were not so much controlled.'

'Aye, and not taxed so heavily,' John said gloomily.

'They wish to bring back the old days, you mean?' Miles asked.

'Did you not find disaffection while you were in the country?' Dick asked.

'A little, yes. But people are not so close to events, they do not feel the effects so speedily.'

'When they do, there will be more plots, and more attempts such as this fellow Wogan,' John prophesied.

'What is this?' Miles asked, managing to conceal the dismay he felt that Wogan was known to these men.

'A fellow claiming to be one of Charles Stuart's officers who is recruiting soldiers to the north of London, mostly in Hertfordshire and Middlesex,' Dick said, laughing.

'A rising? What does he hope to do?' Miles queried, calculating that his display of curiosity would be looked on as normal, and desperately anxious to learn what he could.

'Whatever he hopes, he will not achieve it,' John said confidently. 'He is being watched. He cannot move far without our knowing all about it. We but wait until as many rebels as he can gather are committed, and then we move against them.'

'Will there be many?'

'I doubt if he will raise more than a dozen. But they must be known, and this way of learning who is ready to act against us serves as well as any other.'

There was no more conversation on the matter, as John and Dick began to talk of a new Act Parliament was discussing, and Miles could not prolong the discussion without drawing attention to his interest in it. Fortunately for him, the earlier outburst from Faithful had made several people uncomfortable, and the party began to break up early. Miles took the opportunity to slip away fairly quickly, conscious of the pleading look in Cherry's eyes, warring with her apparent cheerfulness as she bade him farewell. He bit back the suggestion that he return later, and left somewhat hastily.

As he walked along to his lodgings, he reminded himself sternly that he had work to do that night, he could not afford to waste it in dalliance. He had as yet obtained no help directly from Cherry in his work, apart from the company he met at her house. He had no excuse to continue visiting her alone, and he was already feeling regretful that he had tried to use her to obtain information against her friends. Also a deciding factor, his association with her could damage his own cause. He had more than slight reason to be suspicious of her, and she might well be working for Parliament, and be protected by it, which would explain her apparent immunity from punishment when she so flagrantly, and to the knowledge of several of them, it seemed, disobeyed its edicts. He had no doubt that both Dick and John were her lovers, and possibly several more of the men who were constantly at her house. The facade of respectable gatherings was strong, and Miles was certain that many of the guests were genuinely merely friends, but the men normally outnumbered the women, and many of the unattached ones showed particular attentions to Cherry, above those required for a hostess.

He marvelled not only that she could flout convention so by holding her frequent parties without the protection of a male relative as host, but also that she could attract avowed Puritans to them. Not least was her triumph in retaining the friendship of so many women.

Arriving at his lodgings, Miles put these thoughts out of his mind. He must warn Edward Wogan that he was under surveillance. It was not possible to set off immediately, for it would occasion comment if he did so. But he had to contrive to reach Barnet unobtrusively. He dare not simply ride out, for if it became known, and connected with the conversation that evening, he would henceforth be a marked man.

He slept for a few hours, and was up long before dawn. It took some considerable time for him to rub his skin with a judicious mixture of walnut juice and a red dye, then hide his own luxuriant hair under a grey wig dressed in a short, severe fashion. He dressed in plain homespun breeches and coat, and took a rough cloak to throw over it, clapping a tall crowned hat on his head.

Satisfied that he looked the part of a rustic, though reasonably prosperous farmer, he went to hire a horse from the postmaster, leaving his own speedier animal behind.

It was just getting light when he set off, taking the Cambridge road, and not turning westwards until he was several miles out of London, but then making for Barnet and the house where he had earlier met Wogan.

At this house he was shown into the room where the owner, a Mr. Pool, was busy with his accounts. Miles quickly explained his mission, and the reason for his disguise, which had prevented Mr. Pool from recognising him.

'Where is Wogan? Can you contact him?'

'Not now,' Mr. Pool answered worriedly. 'He is gone towards St. Albans, with his men, and I know not where he intends to stay.'

'How many men has he?' Miles asked.

'Barely twenty. He is hoping to recruit a few more, but he has had so little success here that I do not have much hope for him.'

'Then I must ride after him.'

'Will you stay and dine with us?'

'I thank you, but no. 'Tis best no one remarks my visit to you. As 'tis, I will be taken as some business acquaintance.'

They parted, with Mr. Pool's good wishes ringing in Miles' ears, and the promise of help if there were aught he could do. Miles rode for St. Albans, but found no trace of Wogan until he reached the town. There, at the inn where he rested for a meal, he found a man who had seen a troop of horsemen riding out on the Bedford road earlier that morning. Miles set off in pursuit, but it was almost dark when he came up with the men.

They were riding along singing cheerfully, and took no notice of Miles as he urged his horse past the small column. At its head rode Wogan and a young boy, scarcely more than sixteen. Miles reined in beside them.

'I would have speech with you, Mr. Wogan,' he said quietly, and Wogan gave him a startled glance.

'What is't you wish?' he asked after a slight pause.

'I am flattered that you do not see through my disguise. Miles Talbot.'

'To be sure! I thought your voice familiar. You are mightily changed. Have you come to join me after all?'

'Not so. To warn you that your

activities are known to Parliament, and they plan to take you soon.'

Edward Wogan did not seem unduly surprised. 'I have not tried especially hard to keep my activities a secret,' he said, laughing. 'One cannot recruit an army if no one is to know on't!'

'Methinks they know more than you would care for. Even to the names and descriptions of the men you have recruited.'

'What of it? These men are brave fellows, willing to risk all. They do not shrink from being known for their true beliefs and allegiances.'

'But you are few in number. Will you risk all by bravado? Do you not take any precautions? Like this you are easy prey for a troop of Parliament's army. Where are you heading? Why not send the men in twos and threes? They can do nought but harm for the moment by staying together.'

'We show our colours. We need more recruits, and will not get them by passing in secret.'

'You stand to lose all these by passing so openly.'

'Hist! Colonel, I beg pardon, but I hear horses ahead!'

It was the young boy who had continued to ride the far side of Wogan while Miles had been speaking to him. Miles threw him a swift glance, and listened hard. The boy was right, there were sounds ahead that indicated several horses; slight snorts, the jingle of harness, yet no sound of hooves. It was almost dark, and they were approaching a small wood. There was no way round apart from the road which had steep banks to either side except where it passed through the wood.

'Methinks an ambush,' Miles whispered softly. 'We must rush them and break through, and if they seem not too numerous turn and attack as they pursue.'

Wogan has reached the same conclusion, relying on the element of surprise to break through any barrier. Swiftly orders were passed back, and the men closed ranks, riding in the full width of the narrow road. On a word, they spurred their horses to a canter, and then a gallop, and though several horsemen came out of the trees to attempt to intercept them, they broke through, losing only one man whose horse was cut down beneath him.

Miles peered from side to side in the gathering darkness as they charged past, and estimated that there was roughly the same number of men in the attempted ambush as in Wogan's troop. When they had drawn clear of the trap, Miles gave the order to turn, and the troop, inexperienced and undisciplined though it was, performed the manoeuvre creditably, halting their mounts and wheeling them with the minimum of confusion.

Wogan and Miles quickly pushed their way to the front, and their men stood firm behind them. They were still in the shade of the trees, and the surprised ambushers, somewhat discomforted by their failure, had started on a ragged pursuit of the men they imagined would still be fleeing from them. Miles heard the irresolute commands of their leader in the distance, but could not distinguish exactly what was ordered. As the first few men approached, they were thrown into confusion as they perceived the troop awaiting them. Some rode on and attacked, others stopped, while some of the more timid swerved away into the shelter of the trees.

Wogan gave the order to charge, and before the other group could reorganise, it found itself entangled with the men it had hoped to ambush.

The fighting was fierce but short, as the men under Wogan slashed with their swords at the scattered soldiers. Without formation, without the drill they were accustomed to, they were lost, and though a few of them fought bravely and intelligently, the solid block of Wogan's force soon had them routed. Several were wounded, a few killed, and the rest dispersed in considerable disarray. Wogan called off those of his men who would have pursued the remnants of their attackers, and they rode on until they judged it safe to pause and take stock.

'Well done, my friends, well done indeed! 'Sdeath, if you behave so bravely there is none to match you in all England!' Wogan cried.

''Twas indeed a brave showing,' Miles agreed, but added with a note of caution, 'even though we had the advantage of surprise.'

As the men, most of them young and inexperienced, began to talk of the fight and compare their sensations, Wogan said under cover of the general noise, 'We were fortunate, my dear Talbot.'

'Aye, and not like to be so again. The Parliament will smart under this defeat, and send a larger troop to make certain of you next time.'

'Methinks 'twould be better to send the men in small groups, as you suggested.'

'I do not wish to cast discouragement

on your attempt,' Miles said slowly, 'but there is little likelihood of a force strong enough to defy the army. Why not make for Scotland, and then those who think to fight likewise can join you there?'

'Aye. 'Tis the end of one way, but you are right. Not one in ten that I have asked has been willing to join me, and they were all devoted Royalists that I asked!'

'They have too much to lose. 'Tis hard to accept for those of us that have chosen differently, but not so hard to understand.'

'Well, my thanks to you for your help. You risked a great deal on your own account to come and warn us. I trust your mission will not suffer. You are certain you will not join us?'

Miles shook his head. 'I do not fear to have been recognised. Even you did not, and 'twas almost dark when we came upon them. But I wish you all good fortune, and hope to hear of you in Scotland. Now I must bid you farewell, and ride back to London.'

'Will you not stay with us overnight? In the dark, and with the soldiers about, you will be in danger.'

'I must risk that. I dare not be absent for too long at this point, there is so much to be done.'

With more expressions of goodwill they parted, and Miles started back along the road towards the place of ambush. He reasoned that the soldiers would either have ridden off, after their failure, or be coming after them. He did not fear a meeting with them, and in the event he did not have one. He rode for several hours, and put up for the night at a small inn a mile or so out of St. Albans. Rising early, he was off before it was light, and passed the town while it was yet dark. He made good progress, and rode cross country so that he could approach London from the Cambridge road, in case he was seen and remembered. The short winter day was closing in when he entered the City, and by the time he reached his lodgings it was fully dark. Wearily he changed out of his rustic clothes, and removed as much of the colouring that he could from his skin. He was still several shades darker than his natural colour, and ruefully wondered whether he would be able to keep out of the sight of his Parliamentary acquaintances, who would be suspicious if they saw him so.

7

Miles was able to avoid Cherry and her friends for the next week or so, until his skin had returned to its normal hue. He was busy on the work of the Sealed Knot, visiting, organising, and encouraging.

Then, in the middle of the month of December, the City was agog with the news that the Parliament of the Saints, as it was usually known, had been dismissed by Cromwell. Miles made his way that evening to Cherry's hoping to learn more, and he was not disappointed.

Cherry greeted him with a calm she did not feel, for his absence, much longer than usual, had disturbed her, and she fretted to know what had become of him.

'I wondered if you had forgotten us,' she said gaily, as she went into the parlour with him. 'Dick, here is the truant, but I'll warrant he comes only to hear what has been happening!'

'How could I possibly admit that?' Miles asked, laughing into her eyes. 'I have been busy, for my affairs became complicated.'

'I can hazard a guess as to their nature,' Dick said meaningly, and Miles saw Cherry glance quickly at him, then look away in slight confusion. She covered it admirably.

'If you do not tell us your secrets, Mr. Talbot, I shall forbid you the house!'

'Mayhap you would forbid me if you knew them!' he retorted, with truth hidden from his audience. But they merely laughed, and he was soon engrossed in a discussion of the day's events with Dick and several other men, some of them also dismissed Members.

'It worked exactly as planned,' one of these, whom Miles did not recognise, was saying gloatingly.

'We certainly took the others by

surprise, meeting so early in the morning.'

'But your resignation, I understand that it does not apply to all of you?' the merchant Mr. Aston said.

'There were fifty signatures. Colonel Sydenham had hoped for a few more, but the others will come when they see which way the wind is blowing. As soon as there are over half, they will take effect.'

'What will happen now?' asked another man, a merchant by the look of him, Miles thought.

'Ah, that we must wait and see,' Dick answered prudently.

'It cannot be denied that the people were getting restive under the rule of Barebones and his friends.'

'True, and the resignation of the whole of us was the only way.'

'Speak for yourself, traitor Ashford!'

It was Faithful Denham, who had entered during the previous few remarks.

'Do you disagree then?' someone

asked him, and he spluttered with indignation.

''Twas a despicable trick that they thought to play on us! If they did not fear to be defeated in open argument, why meet secretly, at such an early hour, and illegally pass this false resignation?'

'There was nought illegal about it. The Speaker was there, as you well know.'

'But we were prevented from entering when we arrived at the usual time!'

'You should have risen earlier,' Dick said unsympathetically.

'You are sly, wicked devils, and God will surely punish you for your perfidious doings!'

'Do not bemoan your lost dignity, Faithful. This is not the end of Parliaments. Cromwell has promised that there will be another one soon, and this time elected. You will be able to see whether the people desire you and your restrictions.'

'Are you daring to complain at the

rules we would impose, for the good of the people who know no better?'

'I am saying that they would not have borne it for a great while longer. Already there are murmurs against us. There have been Royalist risings and plots. They will increase in importance unless we behave with due regard for the wishes of the people.'

'Dick Ashford, these people know not what to do!' Faithful said, anguish in his voice. 'We seek but to show them the way.'

'So have others before us tried to go against the will of the people. It did not do King Charles much good, for he lost his head defying the people!'

''Tis all a scheme by that arch fiend Cromwell, to gain power for himself! I hear that he is thinking of setting himself up as ruler.'

'Is that true?' Mr. Aston enquired in some surprise.

'Oh, yes, 'tis true,' Faithful said venomously. 'He would rule alone, and become a King!'

'He would have my support if he did,' Dick declared, and this so infuriated Faithful that he fumed speechlessly for a while, and then stalked out of the room.

Cherry had been standing silently by during the argument, and she moved after Faithful, but either she could not persuade him to return, or had not tried, judging the mood of both Faithful and her other guests to be such that they preferred to be apart, for she returned soon alone.

There was little other talk that evening, taken up as everyone was by the strange events of the day, and full of speculations as to the outcome. The Members who had signed the resignation seemed to know something, but they were silent on the topic of the future, and despite straight questions, could not be drawn into statements or speculations.

Miles felt that he had learned all he could, and he found himself tense with desire for Cherry. He was almost resolved to ask her whether he could stay that night, when he noticed her many attentions to John Taunton. He watched jealously, scarcely able to conceal his emotions, but she seemed to be paying unnecessary attention to Taunton, and Miles was unable to do more than exchange a few words with her. She seemed to be avoiding private conversation with him deliberately, and he rejected the idea of attempting to outstay the other guests, as he had done in the past. It was not only his caution that told him he was running into danger, but the fear that he might find out for certain that someone else, most likely Taunton, was more favoured. So he left fairly early, not able to tell from Cherry's manner as she bade him farewell what her feelings were.

She was in fact thoroughly confused. She desired him as keenly as ever, but his sudden reappearance at such a time strengthened her convictions that there was an ulterior motive for his visits. If he truly was a spy she feared that in her state of desperate longing she would be incapable of guarding her tongue, and would unwittingly provide him with the information he sought. Exactly what that was she still could not decide, but thought it likely that the master spy, Thurloe, would be anxious to know the reactions of the dismissed Members, and discover any plans of retaliation or rebellion amongst them.

Miles spent the next few days haunting the taverns that Dick Ashford and his friends frequented, and found them constantly there, and ready to talk of the recent events. They were in general moderate men, unlike Faithful Denham, and regretted that the extremists had gained control.

''Twas not what Cromwell intended,' one of them said to Miles. 'He hoped for sensible reforms, but they made things impossible.'

'Such as abolishing the Court of Chancery?' Miles suggested.

'Indeed yes, when there was no other court for the cases to be sent to! Then the last refusal, to accept the report of their own committee and abolish tithes, meant that no church could be state endowed! This was something Cromwell desired greatly. He could not be expected to countenance such foolishness.'

'What is he like to do now? I hear rumours that he might be set up as King.'

'There have been such rumours for a good many months. When his portrait was set up in the Royal Exchange in May, surmounted by three crowns, many thought that was what he intended, but I would take my oath that he does not wish for the Crown.'

Dick Ashford was listening. 'Aye. The Army have long advocated it. And now Lambert favours it, but not Oliver!' he declared.

'I thought Lambert desired an elected Parliament?'

'Yes, he still holds that view, but now wants a King also. Oh, not one with supreme powers such as the Stuarts tried to wield, but one that would be subject to the power of Parliament,' Dick explained.

'And he has the support of the Army for this?'

'Indeed yes. They want to see Cromwell in power.'

'And no one can exercise power without the support of the Army,' Miles said musingly. 'Has no one else that support?'

'No. Cromwell has tried to renounce the power he held, but he will take it up again when he sees that the country depends on him,' Dick said confidently.

'But not as King?'

'There are other titles,' Dick said, and Miles nodded in agreement.

Soon after this the talk switched to the anger of the Members who had not been in the dawn resignation, and had found themselves locked out of St. Stephen's Chapel by the soldiers.

'You were at Mistress Weston's house the other night, were you not, when Faithful Denham was displaying his

140

anger?' Dick asked.

'Indeed yes. I have frequently seen him roused to great passion, but never so much as then,' Miles said.

'The others of his kind are equally furious.'

'What can they do?'

'Nought but fume and rant against us. But we need some more signatures to the resignation. They are coming in slowly, but Denham and his friends are having some effect, causing some of the uncommitted Members to hesitate.'

'You do not fear they will deter too many from signing?'

'No, there will be a majority for us. It but delays matters. But beware Denham's malice. He would revenge himself on any he thinks against him,' Dick warned.

'Even those who are not Members?' Miles asked curiously.

'Aye. Denham does not regard such niceties. If he considers that you do not support his views, and your friendship with me is sufficient to convince him of that, he will do his utmost to wreak vengeance on you. Try to ignore him, not provoke him to anger. He is powerful, being very wealthy.'

'I will heed your warning,' Miles said, smiling gratefully at Dick, though in his heart he did not think that he stood in any danger, and that Dick exaggerated the venom of Faithful, and the risks he himself stood in by his slight friendship with Dick Ashford.

The Parliament of the Saints had been dismissed on Monday, the twelfth of December, and it was very shortly afterwards, on the Friday, that the situation was resolved. Miles had hoped that the Royalists could take action to benefit from the state of confusion, but in the event there was little confusion. As Dick had predicted, there was soon a majority of Members who had signed the resignation, and Lambert's plan was in part adopted. Cromwell became Lord Protector of England.

Once again Miles made his way to Cherry's house, and found the usual people there, and many of the less frequent visitors who had come to hear about the events of the day.

'His Highness took the oath in Westminster Hall,' John Taunton was explaining. ''Tis in accordance with the Instrument of Government, which lays down the way we are to be governed, from this day on.'

'Will there be no Parliament?' someone asked.

'Indeed there will. The first one is to meet on September third next year, and from then on every third year.'

'The third of September?' It was Cherry who spoke.

'Aye, 'tis said to be Cromwell's lucky day.'

'Indeed yes. The battle of Dunbar,' Dick said.

'When my husband was killed,' Cherry murmured, but so softly that only Miles, who was standing next to her, heard. He looked down at her, but could read nothing from her expression, which was blank.

'Also Worcester,' another guest reminded them, and Miles frowned as he recalled the day, with its bitter fighting and final defeat of the King, and his own wound.

'Will it be another nominated Parliament?'

'No, 'twill be elected. There will be four hundred for England and Wales, and thirty each for Scotland and Ireland. They will sit for the counties and the main towns.'

'Free elections?' Mr. Aston queried.

'All who have estates worth two hundred pounds a year, apart from Papists, and those who have rebelled against Parliament here or in Ireland.'

'How long will it sit?'

'Not less than five months in every three years.'

'And in between sessions?'

'There will be a Council to help the Protector rule. Both they and he are appointed for life, and together will fill vacancies as they arise. Thus we will have the advice of the best men in the land for all our business.'

'You know much about this new system, Mr. Taunton,' Mr. Aston commented.

' 'Tis but the result of long deliberation. Lambert has advised on such a document for some time, and those of us in his confidence have often discussed such ideas. 'Tis no hastily prepared document, for the ideas have been tested by argument.'

'Now they are to be tested in practice.'

The discussion then became general, as the guests began to talk together of the new system. Miles noted that Faithful Denham was not present, and he wondered whether the man would accept the situation, or attempt to overthrow the new ruler.

Miles circulated amongst the many guests that night, noting their views, and considering what effect the changes might have on his own work, and the chances of his master recovering the throne. He found general satisfaction that the Barebones' Parliament had been dissolved, and some relief that the strong man Cromwell was again at the head of affairs. But there was some disquiet too.

'I mislike this 'Highness' in his title,' Mr. Aston was saying to some fellow merchants. 'It smacks of royalty, and I suspect Cromwell to be aiming for the crown.'

'You would dislike that?' Miles asked.

'Aye. We did not get rid of one King merely to set another in his place.'

'But he would be chosen by the people,' another man pointed out. 'A very different affair.'

'How long would that last? He has pride in his family like all of us. He would not wish to see his sons passed over for another.'

'But he is not King. We have had Protectors before.'

'And never done well out of them. All this change is bad for trade.'

'I trust we shall see the end of the Days of Humiliation,' a youngish merchant said. 'We cannot afford to close our shops as often as they would have us do.'

Miles felt a light touch on his arm, and turned to see Mistress Anne Aston simpering up at him.

'Well, Mr. Talbot, I have seen little of you the last few months,' she whispered, casting a wary glance at her husband.

He was still deep in the discussion of trading prospects under the Protector's rule, and unaware of his wife's activities.

'You have not always been here when I have,' Miles countered.

'No. My husband does not care for too much visiting. He does not realise that I need young company. But I invited you to visit me, and you have not been. I take that ill of you.'

She pouted, peering up at Miles through her lashes.

'I have been out of London a great deal,' Miles excused himself.

'Fie, sir, that is a poor excuse. You are

here often enough. I begin to think you do not like me as well as you like Cherry Weston!'

'You have a husband who might object to my visits,' he told her, laughing to himself at her inept approach.

'I have said, he does not object to my entertaining my friends. But I cannot entertain in the evenings as Cherry does, for he prefers to be alone then.'

'If you are certain he would not object, I will call, but I have to leave London again soon, and cannot tell how long I shall be absent,' Miles told her, and with this she had to be content, as at that moment her husband declared that it was time to leave.

Cherry had been watching this exchange, and was startled to discover how strongly she was resenting the attentions, innocuous though they seemed, that Miles was paying to Anne Aston. After she had seen her guests out, several of the older ones leaving with the Astons, she found herself sitting beside Miles, with no clear recollection of how she had come to be there.

They chatted for a few minutes on general matters, and Cherry did her utmost to concentrate on what they were saying. But the effort was too great. She suddenly interrupted Miles.

'Will you stay behind tonight, Miles?'

He looked at her steadily for a moment, during which she cursed herself for being so abrupt, and almost panicked that he was about to refuse her. He nodded slightly, however, and continued with what he had been saying, and somehow she recovered her poise, and was able to smile, and leave him to talk with other guests.

Miles sat where she had left him, wondering whether he had been wise. He knew that the question was academic, for he could no more have said no to such a direct request than he could have flown. Gradually all the other guests departed, and at last they were alone. Cherry had half regretted her impulse, but had been unable to prevent herself from uttering the invitation. She determined to avoid all political subjects, and for a time this was possible.

As they lay side by side she asked Miles whether he had yet found an estate.

'Not yet. I have seen one that might be possible, but I have to visit more. I will be leaving London within a few days.'

'Oh! How long will you be gone this time?'

'I cannot tell. If I hear of other properties I will go to see them.'

'If you become a property owner, you will be able to stand for the new Parliament. You said once that you might do that.'

'I might indeed. Once I have bought my property, I can offer myself to the electors of that county.'

'Where is it likely to be? You have not said what area you have a preference for.'

'The midlands or the west, methinks,' he told her. 'But I wonder how like the old Parliament this new one will be?'

'In what way?'

'The desire of its members to impose religious ideas on the people.'

'That will depend on the men elected. 'Tis why men who are not bigoted must be elected!'

He looked at her quickly, and saw that she was ill at ease. She had suddenly realised that she had been incautious in expressing such an opinion, for she still thought that he might be trying to trap her.

'I mean some of the men like Faithful, who are so anxious to forward their own ideas that they do not stop to see whether they are acceptable,' she explained hurriedly.

'Aye. Where was Faithful tonight?'

'I know not. He does not usually miss these evenings, but he may have decided that there would be too much argument if he were here, and been desirous of avoiding that. He means well, even though his manner is disagreeable at times.'

'I find it more comfortable when he is not here, I confess,' Miles said with a laugh.

Cherry merely smiled, and hurriedly went on to talk of less dangerous topics.

Reluctantly, their desire for one another having increased once they had given way to their longing, they parted. Miles promised that he would send to tell Cherry when he returned to London, and while she was urging him to do so, she was telling herself that she must restrain her weakness for him, and not put herself into a dangerous situation again. Miles was thinking very similar thoughts as he slipped quietly out of the house, and he did not see the figure in the dark passage opposite.

As he walked away, keeping close to the wall under the overhanging eaves, this figure moved cautiously after him. Faithful Denham had had an exceedingly long wait, and he was numb with cold, despite his fur lined cloak that was wrapped tightly about him. He had taken up the position late in the evening, and watched most of the guests leave Cherry's house. He had for some time been suspicious that she entertained a lover, and in his fury and frustration over the events of the last week, he hoped that he would discover that this lover was one of his erstwhile fellow Members. Then, he had thought gleefully, he would be able to obtain revenge on at least one of the renegades who had ruined his work.

When the man he expected appeared, he was unable to see in the darkness who it was, for the broad brimmed hat shielded the man's face, and the long cloak disguised his figure. Faithful therefore followed at a distance, but to his intense anger, lost his quarry in the maze of alleys and streets round St. Paul's. After a fruitless search he made his way home, but determined that he would not be defeated. He shuddered at the thought of spending yet more nights in the freezing cold watching the house, and decided that he must employ someone to do this for him. He had briefly considered using his apprentices for the task, but concluded that they might be able to use the knowledge they gained against him. Determined to seek the aid of strangers, he went home to bed, and Miles, unaware that he had been followed did the same.

8

Miles, in consultation with Armorer and the leaders of the Sealed Knot, had determined to visit the King and give a report on all that was happening. He set off a few days after his night with Cherry, and was away for over a month. When he returned to England he had to set out immediately for Lancashire to visit several people with messages from the King.

There was a considerable amount of activity amongst the Royalists in England now. They were beginning to recover hope after the defeat of Worcester, and also the fear that Cromwell might usurp the throne as well as the power of ruler spurred many to efforts on the King's behalf.

Nicholas Armorer was travelling in the northen counties, and Miles was also kept busy there and in the west for some months. It was towards the end of April that he returned to London. As before, he sent word to Cherry, and she sent back to say that she was engaged that night, and could not avoid it, but would be happy to see him at a small party the following night.

Disappointed, having hoped for an immediate invitation, he fretted about his lodgings, then decided to visit Sir Henry Villiers. Sir Henry had moved his own lodgings again, and was near the Inner Temple now. Miles found his way there, and was warmly welcomed by Sir Henry, who called for wine and was very ready to discuss the progress of events.

'The Protector and the Council have issued many ordinances,' he told Miles.

'There seems to be an acceptance that will be difficult to change,' Miles said gloomily.

'I am not so certain. When Cromwell dined with the Lord Mayor in February there was not much enthusiasm in the City for him. People were thankful to be rid of Barebones and his motley crew, but are not hastening to welcome Cromwell.'

'So our plots may stand more chance of success.'

'I think so, even though the attempt in February met with so little success.'

'I heard rumours of this, but no clear details. It was concerted by men who would not consult the Knot.'

'Aye, and foolish men they were! They were free with their talk in the taverns, and 'twas an open secret that they were meeting regularly at the Ship, in Old Bailey. The men Thurloe employs did not need to use much cunning to learn the details!'

'This is like to happen all the time, with enthusiastic hotheads refusing to use patience or caution,' Miles commented ruefully.

'But they had such wild notions! First they would instigate a riot amongst the apprentices, and use it to seize London! As if any could control the London apprentices once they are rioting! These men had little idea of what such a riot could be like.'

'What happened to them?'

'Most were arrested, including Whitley and Ditton, the leaders, but I know there were some that escaped. I hope that they do not concoct other such wild plans.'

'There are similar plots brewing all over the country,' Miles told him. 'Much of it due to the feeling that nought is being done by the leaders the King has appointed.'

'You mean the Knot?'

'Aye. Many feel that 'tis too cautious, and bolder measures are needed.'

'The Knot will never consent to taking risks. I know them too well, and I cannot blame them. I was involved in the Norfolk rising in fifty, and barely escaped with my life. Most of my friends were not so fortunate. If small affairs like that are too frequent, our most likely men are killed or captured, as Wogan was killed in a skirmish in Scotland, or lose the nerve for further risings.'

'Agreed, we need to concert the efforts, but unless the Knot shows itself more active, men will not be content to wait.'

'We must try to persuade them,' Sir Henry said.

' 'Tis not so easy. I have just had four months of talking with them. But enough of that. How is life with you? How is your wife, and the children? Content to remain in Norfolk without you?'

'I pay frequent visits home when I am not needed here,' Sir Henry said, smiling. 'My wife is breeding again, which is a great joy to me. She is a most satisfactory wife in all respects.'

He talked for some time about his family, and Miles was silent, wondering if he would ever himself be able to do the same. He admitted to himself that he would never marry anyone but Cherry, though the prospect of doing that seemed exceedingly remote if she were working for Thurloe and the

Parliamentarians.

Miles hungered for the sight of her, and arrived early at her house the following evening, to find a select group of her friends, mostly the neighbouring merchants, and only John Taunton of the Parliamentary set.

That evening the talk was largely nonpolitical, mostly to do with trade, and the improved prospects now that peace had been made with the Dutch. Anne Aston and several of the younger wives were full of plans to take advantage of the less strict regime to go a'maying in Hyde Park.

'I have never been, for't has been banned since I was a child,' Anne was saying eagerly. 'Cherry, you will come with us, will you not?'

'To be sure I will. I can remember dancing round the maypole when I was a girl, and I would love to do such again.'

'You will have to get up early,' one of the other women warned. 'I know that you lie late in bed, Cherry.'

'I need to stay refreshed for these evenings,' Cherry retorted. 'But I will be certain to rise early, before dawn, and will be there before you all!'

'I know not why you want to do such things,' Mr. Aston said, looking indulgently at his wife.

She smiled at him. 'To make ourselves as beautiful as possible for our husbands.'

'That would be impossible, that you could be more beautiful,' John Taunton said gallantly, and they all laughed, while Anne blushed.

'Are we men to be allowed to join in the revelry?' one of the younger men asked, and the women assured him that all would be welcome to make the party gayer.

'I understood such revelries were banned still?' one timid girl suggested.

'Why, so they are, but no one pays heed to that now. I have heard of hundreds who are planning to go,' Anne reassured her, and they began to make plans.

Some time later Cherry spoke alone with Miles. After asking whether he had had a good journey, and whether he had settled on a property yet, she was silent for a while.

'Will you — ' she broke off, and bit her lip. She had determined not to ask him to stay the night, and here was her rebellious tongue about to do so at the first opportunity.

'Will you join us on May morn?' she said hurriedly, and Miles, who knew perfectly well that she had changed her mind, in what she had been about to say, nodded unsmilingly. He had been fighting the desire to take her in his arms all evening, scarcely restrained by the other guests, and this rebuff hit him like a pail of cold water. He knew that it was silly to visit her while he suspected her, but he longed for her so deeply that he refused to be cautious. However, there was little he could do, and he made his departure early, jealously wondering if John Taunton was to be more fortunate than himself.

On May day, Miles was up long before dawn, and rode out to Hyde Park on the west of London. There were many others going in the same direction, and all dressed in their finest clothes. As well as the richer merchants, there were hundreds of the lesser tradesfolk, and many maids and apprentices. Even the gentry seemed to be joining in the general merriment, and several coaches were being driven to the park.

Anne Aston had explained that they intended to meet at the side nearest St. James's Palace, and Miles found a large party already assembled when he arrived. Cherry was there, dressed in a white taffeta gown embroidered in pink. She smiled up at Miles as he drew rein beside them.

'Leave your mount over there,' she suggested. 'One of my menservants will take care of them.'

Nodding his thanks, Miles delivered his horse into this man's charge, and rejoined the group. They were chatting merrily, and chaffing the latecomers. Soon after Miles had arrived, the party was complete, and they moved further into the park towards a scattered clump of trees.

Anne Aston, much livelier than Miles had seen her previously, was leading the way, accompanied by two of the younger men. When they reached the edge of the trees, she turned and addressed the party.

'First, we must all bathe our faces in the dew,' she said, laughing, and bent down to wet her hands in the long grass. The women followed suit, and emitted cries of pleasure or dismay as the cool dew was transferred to their faces.

'What is it supposed to do for us?' one young girl asked.

'It removes all blemishes, and softens the skin,' Anne replied.

'Then I shall try it on my arms too,' the girl said, and pushing up her sleeves, began to bathe her arms in the moisture.

'I have a mole on my ankle,' another said, and amidst cries of encouragement from the men, slipped off her shoe, and, pretending coyness, turned away to roll down her stocking. She then extended her foot, carefully raising her skirts the smallest way possible for the ankle to be visible.

'Where is the mole? I cannot see it, I vow!' The speaker was kneeling beside her, and at this others tried to find the elusive mark.

'I have one by my knee,' Anne claimed, and pretended to be horrified when she was asked to show it.

Soon the claims of blemishes and the suggestions for bathing them grew wilder and more hilarious. Some genteel struggles were taking place, and a few couples had drifted away from the main group. Cherry had watched it all with a slightly abstracted air, not competing for attention, and Miles had stayed beside her. He bent towards her after a short time.

'I can remember the most delectable

mole,' he whispered. 'I have kissed it often, and think of doing so every day and night.'

She turned quickly towards him, and he glimpsed a look of pure amusement in her eyes, the sort of look she had so often given him, and which attracted him so. But soon it vanished, and he was startled to see a look of pain in her face.

'Cherry, what is it?' he asked in quick concern.

'Nought, I assure you.' She struggled to recover her composure, which was threatened by his company. The effort to deny him, to restrain the longing for him, was worse than anything she had previously experienced.

'Come, we must dance,' Anne Aston called at that moment, and Cherry turned with relief to this diversion. They set about gathering branches, and not having a Maypole, tried to reconstruct the old dance without the ribbons. Using the branches, and encircling a small tree, they danced in the traditional rings. Many of the younger people had never seen the dance, or could not remember it from ten years or more ago, but there were sufficient older people there to provide instruction, and the mistakes caused great hilarity.

Soon they were breathless from the unwonted exertion, and collapsed onto the ground.

'We must choose a Queen for the day,' Anne said, and looked around hopefully. 'Who shall it be?'

Several of the men glanced at Cherry, for they all visited her house, and she seemed a natural leader, as well as being the most beautiful woman there. But before anyone could speak she made her own suggestion.'

'Why, you must be it, of course, Anne.'

'I thought it had to be a maid,' one of the younger unmarried girls said a trifle wistfully.

'I know not what rules there are, but surely we can make our own? Let the

Queen have some attendants,' Cherry suggested.

This was applauded, and Anne, well satisfied, was decked with garlands of flowers as were the girls selected to be her attendants. When this was done, they formed a procession, and made their way back to where the horses and a few coaches waited.

'We have brought food, and will eat there,' Anne declared regally.

For some time the merriment continued, as they ate and drank. All over the park other groups were making merry in much the same way. Milkmaids were selling tankards of milk straight from the cows, and Cherry expressed a wish to try some.

''Tis years since I was able to do so, when I lived in the country,' she explained to Miles as he escorted her across the park to buy the milk. 'And I am not usually up early enough to enjoy it like this, in the cool of the morning.'

'Do you never walk in the parks?' Miles asked in some surprise, for it was a fashionable pastime. 'The cows are here all day.'

'I come sometimes, but not as often as I should,' Cherry replied.

'Will you come with me some day?' Miles said before he had considered whether it was a wise invitation.

'That would be pleasant,' Cherry answered, but at that moment they reached the place where the milk was being served, and neither of them referred to the suggestion again. Miles was debating whether, since so many people knew that he frequented Cherry's house, it would be dangerous to be seen in public with her. Cherry was deciding that she must avoid such expeditions, for the more she saw of Miles the more difficult she found it to be on her guard against him, and to remember that he might be a spy waiting to betray an incautious word.

Gradually the revellers were dispersing, and Cherry bade Miles farewell as she prepared to depart with the Astons, who had brought her in their coach.

Miles rode behind, with some of the other men, and they went towards Charing Cross. Glancing around, Miles was startled to see Faithful Denham standing at the side of the road, glaring venomously after the Astons' coach. He was muttering to himself as they rode past, and did not appear to see the riders, though one of them hailed him.

'Poor Faithful! He has been more than usually morose these last few months, preaching against all forms of pleasure, and declaring that we are all sinners. He appears to have come to view the sinning!'

'To be able to fulminate more knowledgeably about it, no doubt,' another laughed. 'I confess I have been relieved that he has not haunted Mistress Weston's house so assiduously as in the past. He made things uncomfortable many times.'

'Aye. I cannot think why he frequents the company, he detests it so.'

''Tis the moth and the candle. He objects to Mistress Weston's hospitality, and the good company to be found there, but he cannot keep away from her. Have you not seen him gazing at her?'

'But everyone is in love with Mistress Weston! You would not expect Faithful to be immune from a universal disease?' another man put in.

'I do not expect him to have any normal appetites.'

'Oh, it makes me gloomy even to think of him,' someone protested, and they began to talk of other things.

But the next time Miles was at Cherry's, a few days later, Faithful Denham was there, sitting for the most part of the evening in a corner, and talking to no one. The few remarks that were addressed to him he answered so surlily that those guests disposed to be friendly or polite soon left him alone.

That evening there was music, with some of the guests performing, and so there was little time for conversation. Miles managed to speak but a few words with Cherry, and could not avoid the impression that she deliberately kept out of his way. He saw jealously that John Taunton was much in favour, and helpless with longing, left the house as soon as he decently could, but in company with others so that he had no private speech with Cherry. She seemed relieved to see him go, and he wondered, as he walked along to his lodgings, whether he was any better than Faithful, any better able to protect himself from burning at the candle flame. He wondered whether he ought to give up seeing her, but decided that, difficult as it made life for him, his work made it essential to maintain the contacts he had in the Parliamentarian party. If he stopped going to Cherry's it would occasion comment, and this he must avoid.

A couple of days later, he visited Sir Henry, and heard some disturbing news.

'Those madmen I told you of, who were plotting the riot of the apprentices in February have a further plot,' Sir

Henry said after greetings had been exchanged.

'What is't this time?'

'Nothing less than the assassination of the Protector.'

'What? Are they indeed crazy? Have they asked your blessing or advice on this?'

'Oh no. Despite the fact that John Gerard, the leader, knows full well that the Knot needs to direct and sanction plots, he has said no word of it to us.'

'How did you hear of it?'

'Because we heard that the Council are planning to arrest them.'

'How do you come by such information?' Miles asked a little sceptically. 'Have you an informer?'

'Not precisely. It came to us through an agent, a woman who has close connections with Parliament and the Army.'

'A woman? I have not heard of such a one.'

'No, she is not an accredited agent. The arrangement has been a private one between us. I have known her for many years, and circumstances put her in the way of discovering such secrets. She passes them on to me, and I have several times been able to warn people and save them from arrest.'

'Her information is reliable?'

'I have always found it so.'

'Who is she?' Miles asked curiously.

'She has made me promise not to reveal her name to anyone else,' Sir Henry said slowly. 'She fears that it might cause danger to her and to the cause if her double life were known. I am her only contact, and she prefers it that way.'

'It seems risky for her. Forgive me, but if aught happened to you?'

'That is a hazard we must accept. But can you make contact with Gerard and pass on the warning? I understand they plan to kill the Protector on the eleventh of this month, as he goes from Whitehall to Hampton Court. They must not do it.'

'Indeed no. 'Twould alienate too

many people. Do they not consider this?'

'They consider only that with Cromwell out of the way, England will fall like a ripe plum into their hands.'

'Then they know too little about the Army, and the other leaders, if they think that would be allowed to happen.'

'I will give you their directions.'

'Thank you. I will see them at once.'

9

Miles soon contrived a meeting with Gerard, the leader of this new plot, and presented his credentials.

'I have come to ask you to reconsider your plans,' he said. 'To assassinate the Protector will turn people against all Royalists.'

'But he is the stumbling block. No one else in his following has the authority to lead,' Gerard explained.

'That does not help us. Unless we can get the King established, the situation would only get worse.'

'I do not see that. With Cromwell gone, the King could come back when he wished, and none to say him nay.'

'There are many, not only in the Army, but the Puritans, who would resist. I know full well that there is little enough positive support in the country at this time for a landing by the King to be successful, 'Twould simply lead to more useless fighting, and undo all the progress we are making.'

'In other words, my plan conflicts with yours, and you wish me to step down so as to leave you with a clear field? Is that it?'

'No so. We are exploring many ways, but most importantly we are trying to win support so that the King can rely on many people when he does come back. This action, whether successful or not, would cost us much of the support we are already gaining amongst moderate people.'

'I cannot agree. There is great need for action. The Sealed Knot does nought, and people are wondering why. They will lose hope the longer time that passes without some sign that the leaders are leading!'

'I agree it seems as though nought is being done, but 'tis not so. A great deal is being done in a quiet way, and when the time is ripe action will be taken. But we cannot afford to move unsuccessfully, and dissipate our support and our hopes. It was agreed with the King that all plans should be put first to the Knot, and be carried out only with their approbation and under their general guidance. Thus we can direct the many efforts into what we think the best ways of proceeding.'

Gerard looked at him for a time, and then shook his head.

'But they are doing nought to encourage the people who desire the King's return, but who are not involved in the plotting, and who do not know that something is being done. What I plan will do that, and I cannot accept that it would make the situation worse.'

Miles laughed. 'You seem unwilling to think what would happen if you were successful. The Army would institute many repressive measures, and many people now at liberty would be arrested. Do not underestimate Thurloe. He has an excellent spy system. How do you think I came to know of your plans?'

'I confess I had been wondering who had been to consult with the Knot.'

'No one has. But someone has been indiscreet, for the Council know all about it, and 'twas only that one of our agents discovered it from them that we heard of it.'

'What?' Gerard was shaken out of his calm. 'You say that all is known?'

'Aye, and arrests will be made unless you give up the idea and, for your own safety, leave the country.'

'I do not believe you.'

'I am but issuing a warning. I can see that I will not dissuade you from your attempt by appealing to your reason, but I know well that you will not be allowed to succeed. You will be permitted to incriminate yourselves sufficiently, and then an example will be made of you and your friends.'

'With evidence provided by the Knot, no doubt?' Gerard sneered.

Miles looked at him coolly. 'I resent that implication, sir, and would call you to give satisfaction for't if 'twere not that to fight might bring too much unwelcome attention to us. But if we meet in another country one day, I will remember it.'

'Bound by orders, no doubt! Or fear.'

'Are you trying to provoke me? You will not succeed unless I consider that removing you would be for the good of the cause we are both supposed to be serving. That is another warning you had best heed!'

Clenching his fists tightly to restrain himself from attacking the man, Miles swung on his heel and left Gerard, furious that the man had been able to insult him, and for the sake of the King's cause he had been forced to swallow the insult. He strode along unseeingly for some time, then the worry of what Gerard might do, and the harm this could cause displaced his personal anger.

After further consideration, he called on Sir Richard Willys and told him all that had passed. 'Could you use your influence with the man?' he asked. 'The more warnings he receives the more the chance that he might take some heed of them.'

Sir Richard promised to use what influence he had, and said that he would consult with his fellow members of the Knot.

'You are right that we must stop such madmen.'

'Aye, but I could not help agreeing with some of his feelings. We are not doing enough to keep the spirits of our supporters high.'

'We cannot afford to risk all before the time is ripe.'

'I know that, and argued so with Gerard. But I begin to wonder, as I know many people do, what else we might do,' Miles answered slowly.

'You criticise us?'

'I begin to feel we are overcautious.'

'Would you have us behave as this fellow, and try to kill the leaders of the Council, mayhap?'

'By no means. Yet there is an immense desire in the country for action. If we made more efforts to concert and organise it, I am sure that we could plan a rising that would have a high chance of success.'

'The time has not yet come for that. We need more support.'

'Are you certain that it is not there, waiting for a lead to be given? I argued with Gerard that he could not expect the whole country to fall at Charles' feet once Cromwell were out of the way, and I know that to be so. It needs organisation, more contacts, people in every county and every town who will raise support when the word is given. With such support, we might begin to plan for a rising.'

'We have considered such possibilities, believe me, Mr. Talbot,' Sir Richard said a trifle coldly. 'The King's authority rests with us, and we shall decide what 'tis best to do.'

Miles shrugged, and soon departed, feeling considerable dissatisfaction with the whole business. He wondered whether he was being unduly affected by his frustration over Cherry, but believed that the Knot was acting too cautiously.

The day before the planned assassination, Miles visited Sir Henry to see whether he had heard any more.

'There have been no arrests until now,' Sir Henry told him, 'though our agent is convinced that something is planned. She cannot get the details, but says that the men round the Protector are fully aware of the plot. All she can discover is that they say it cannot succeed.'

'I wish the fools would give up and leave London. They are bound to be arrested if they do not.'

'Come to me tomorrow. The agent may have more news then.' Sir Henry suggested.

'We leave it late. Tomorrow Cromwell travels to Hampton, and surely the arrests will be made before then?'

'There is nought we can do to prevent them.'

'What if your agent is wrong, and

there is no knowledge of the plot other than a general sort? What if they do not know all the men?'

'You can discount that idea. This woman is one of the most successful and accurate agents we have ever employed. She has never been wrong in the information she has given us. Do not fear that the assassination will be permitted, and the cause harmed.'

'I trust you are right. Till tomorrow, then. I will come early.'

The next day Miles was with Sir Henry soon after it was light, to find that the agent had already been to him.

'The Protector will travel by river, and the plotters are to be foiled,' Sir Henry informed him.

'Then there are to be no arrests? That I do not believe.'

'It appears that more evidence is wanted. They seem to think that if this attempt is foiled, another will be made, and they will pounce then.'

'They are confident about it,' commented Miles. 'The Protector is in danger while they wait.'

'That is true, but probably no more than at any time, for there could be many fanatics waiting to murder him.'

There was no more to be gained by further discussion, and Miles left, but could not stop worrying about the plot. After he had breakfasted in a nearby tavern, he made his way to Gerard's house, and took up a position in a tavern nearby, where he could keep the door of the house under observation. It was some time before his patience was rewarded, but eventually Gerard appeared, wearing a long dark cloak, and set off in the direction of the Bridge.

Miles followed at a cautious distance. Gerard was walking quickly, and casting many suspicious glances around. Miles was able to keep out of view, staying well back and ensuring that there were always many other people between him and his quarry. Gerard turned down Fish Street Hill, and began to cross the Bridge. Here the traffic was so congested that progress was slow. Miles saw Gerard, after another look round, hastily dive into one of the shops which lined the side of the bridge.

At that moment two carts travelling in opposite directions became entangled as their wheels locked, and the drivers began to sling invective at each other, appearing to be in no hurry to release the carts and remove the obstruction in the roadway, which was very narrow. Miles joined the interested crowd that collected round the carts, and watched for Gerard's reappearance. In the meantime he listened with appreciation to the comments of both participants and spectators, who were vociferously disparaging the looks, parentage, and probable futures of the two drivers.

Out of the corner of his eye Miles perceived Gerard emerge from the shop. He carried a bundle, long and thin, and Miles pursed his lips. It was as he had feared. Gerard had not abandoned his attempt at assassination.

Gerard hurried over to the far side of the Bridge, and casually extricating himself from the crowd about the carts, Miles followed. At the south end of the Bridge, Gerard turned aside and entered an inn. Miles hovered nearby. Then Gerard came out from the stableyard, riding a mangy horse. Waiting only to be certain of the road he took, Miles went speedily to another inn and hired a horse for himself. Then he set to trail Gerard, who had taken the road towards Lambeth.

Miles judged that Gerard was aiming to reach the bank of the river by Lambeth, and from there attempt to shoot the Protector as he travelled by barge from Whitehall. He hoped that there were no others of the plotters stationed elsewhere along the river, but if there were, he could do nothing. Gerard at least he could stop, and possibly prevent his arrest as well as his attempt at assassination.

Here in the open country it was more

difficult to trail Gerard without rousing his suspicions, and Miles had to keep a long distance behind. He could see Gerard, and maintained as great a distance as he dared between them. But now that he had left the City behind, Gerard did not seem to be so concerned. He rode along at a moderate speed, and as there were several other travellers Miles was not too conspicuous.

Arriving at Lambeth, Gerard stabled his horse at an inn, and then made his way towards the river. Miles, having seen to the disposal of his own mount, followed. Gerard was standing on a path at the side of the river, in a spot where he was hidden from the village of Lambeth behind him, and anxiously scanning the river. Miles looked across towards the northern bank, but there was nothing nearby at the moment that could be the Protector's barge.

Miles walked up to Gerard, and greeted him.

'Well met, Mr. Gerard.'

Gerard spun round, and Miles saw the pistol partly concealed by the voluminous cloak.

'Well now, my friend, are you expecting some challenger to a duel?'

'What do you here?' Gerard asked furiously.

'Is it not a free road? I but take the air, as you are doing.'

'You are spying on me!'

Miles laughed. 'Correct, my friend. I am also going to prevent you from what you have intended.'

'Oh no you do not.' Gerard swung the pistol menacingly towards Miles. 'You have done your best to betray the matter to the authorities, but you have not succeeded, and will not!'

'Do you propose to shoot me to prevent it?' Miles asked indicating the pistol.

'Aye, if argument will not deter you from your interference.'

'Then let us see what argument will do. What do you hope to gain by this murder?'

'We have argued this before,' Gerard said wearily. 'We need action, and Cromwell is too powerful to destroy any other way.'

'If I agree that more action is needed, and could obtain the King's consent to it, would you be willing to work with me and with others to produce it?'

'What? Are you considering deserting the Knot?'

'No, but I do see that more could mayhap be done. But there will be no success without some authority at the centre to coordinate the plans.'

''Tis but a trick. The men of the Knot would not agree. They are too timid, and fearful for their own skins. We are not.'

'Sensible caution is a necessary attribute for fighters,' Miles observed.'

''Tis a name for cowardice.'

They continued to argue for some time, but Miles could not persuade Gerard that there was any hope of more action under the present leaders of the conspiracy. He was determined to follow his own plans.

While they had been talking, they had both been watching the river, and Gerard at last spotted the barge he had been awaiting. Miles had seen it too. It was not far away, and being rowed rapidly towards them, near to the bank on which they stood as the rowers approached the bend in the river.

Gerard moved away from Miles, and took up a position where he had an uninterrupted view of the barge for a considerable distance. Miles stayed where he was, a few yards back.

The barge came nearer, and was almost level with Gerard. He raised the pistol, but before he could take aim Miles leapt forward, and catching Gerard about the body swung him round. Gerard stumbled, and Miles was able to grasp the pistol and wrench it away. He tossed it out into the water, and the faint splash it made was scarcely noticeable. Gerard was struggling furiously, but Miles was strong and had a firm hold on him. He managed to twist Gerard's arms behind him, and held them while Gerard gasped with pain.

'I do not like assassins, but understand your feelings,' Miles said quietly into Gerard's ear. 'Will you give up your plans? Will you join us in working together for a restoration?'

'You devil! 'Sblood, I will pay you back for this. You have ruined the best chance we had!'

'Will you not answer my questions?' Miles persisted.

'No! I will never work with one so treacherous as you! You are no friend of the King to prevent me from killing his enemy.'

'I do not like murder.'

'We are at war, 'tis no ordinary killing!'

''Tis murder, and you would have the King stained with the blame for't.'

'Nonsense! He had nought to do with it!'

'How are we to tell the uncommitted people that? How will they know, when 'tis his agents that do the deed?'

'I care not. You have destroyed this opportunity, but do not think that you have silenced us!'

'I do not think that. I merely wonder why the authorities have not done so before now. They will, be sure on't. Will you not save your skin by fleeing abroad?'

'So, you would have me a coward too?'

'Why not go to the King, and put your arguments to him? He would mayhap be able to convince you, and there would be nought to prevent you from returning when the matter has been forgotten, and working for the King's cause again.'

'Have you any more tricks? Any more blandishments to hold out to me?'

'No. For I see that you are as stubborn as a mule! I have tried to prevent you from damaging the King's cause, and at the same time save yourself. If you will not listen, I can do no more. I must then let events take their course, and mayhap you will be convinced when Thurloe has his say!'

With that, Miles threw Gerard roughly to the ground, and turned to retrace his steps, fuming with anger that he had not succeeded in convincing the man, but with a slight glow of satisfaction that on this occasion at least, he had retrieved matters for the King.

He rode back to London, and left the bitterly angry Gerard to follow. On the way he was planning to make a visit to the King and try to persuade him to allow more actively inclined men a say in the conspiracy, for he realised much of the truth in Gerard's assertions that support would be lost if hope were not soon provided for the King's supporters.

10

For some days there was no further news of Gerard or his fellow plotters. They had not been arrested, and Miles again began to wonder whether Thurloe and his spies really knew as much about the affair as Sir Henry claimed. The members of the Knot were not especially interested now that they thought the danger was over, and were planning further talks with Royalists in the western counties.

Miles spent a couple of evenings at Cherry's house, but discovered nothing from those who were close to the government. All that happened as a result of these evenings was further frustration for himself, since Cherry made little attempt to converse with him. He was almost on the verge of begging her to allow him to stay, and on the Saturday evening stayed late, after most of the other guests had left.

John Taunton and Faithful Denham were amongst the few that remained. The talk was desultory, though Faithful livened matters up when he began to fulminate against the May Day revels at the beginning of the month.

'We will stop such abandoned mischief,' he declared, and John asked quickly who he meant would stop it.

'You may be in power for the time, John Taunton, but the ungodly shall be defeated, and the righteous will come to rule.'

'Do you mean another Parliament of the Saints? No, the Protector had enough of Barebones and the others last time. He will not tolerate such impudence again.'

'He will have no say in the matter. The elections are to be free, and we will have as much right to stand as you. Methinks you will be surprised when you see how many of the people support us!'

'I think not,' John murmured quietly.

Cherry managed to draw Faithful aside, and soon he took his leave. All the other guests apart from Miles and John Taunton also began to say their goodbyes. Cherry was talking with one of these when she happened to catch sight of Miles standing behind him. Finishing her farewells, she turned and smiled, somewhat anxiously, at Miles.

'Farewell, Mr. Talbot. I hope to see you here next week.'

Miles had no alternative but to take the dismissal, conscious that John Taunton was watching them.

'I shall be leaving London again soon,' he contrived to say quietly to Cherry.

'Oh?' He thought that she seemed dismayed, but then she recovered her smile. 'Then I hope you will find time to visit me before you go.'

Miles left with the other guests, and escaped from them as soon as possible, but he was unwilling to go home. He walked towards St. Pauls, and in the moonlight inspected the fallen masonry at the south end. It had collapsed early in January when the government had removed scaffolding placed there much earlier in preparation for making repairs. Many people had seen it as a portent, but Miles regarded it simply as reflecting his own miserable condition with regard to Cherry.

He went northwards and walked in the fields beyond the City bounds all night. When the early summer dawn came, he had decided that he must forget Cherry. She could no longer be of any use in serving as an introduction to the men around Cromwell, for he already knew many of them, and could without suspicion seek them out himself. He left undecided the question of whether he would visit her again, whether it would be more noticeable if he did, or if he did not. For the time, he must set off to visit the King. There was nothing to keep him in London once the decision was made, and he turned, astonished to see how far he had come, and made his way back towards the City.

He intended to call on Sir Henry before he went home, and inform him that he was about to go abroad, and so he made his way towards Temple Bar. He turned into Middle Temple Lane, which was the shortest way to Sir Henry's lodgings, and stopped short. There, only a few yards in front of him, was Cherry, dressed as he had once before seen her dressed in this very place. She was hurrying along, her shabby dress helping to disguise her lovely figure, but there could be no mistake.

Miles watched, remembering the previous time when he had followed her here, and wondering what it was that brought her. He was certain that she had spent the night with John Taunton. He had been spending most of his own night trying to dismiss the fact and the jealousy it aroused from his mind. Was she now going to another lover? Somehow he did not believe it. But what was she doing there, dressed so?

She turned aside into a narrow passageway, and Miles stepped forward. Before he had decided whether to follow her and try and solve the mystery, however, a sharp scream, suddenly stifled, came from the passageway she had entered.

He broke into a run, and moments later rounded the corner. Cherry was struggling with two men, while another stood watching.

Miles drew the sword he always carried, and lunged at the onlooker who was in between him and the others, and the man fell to the ground with scarce a cry while Miles leaped over him and, seizing the man who held Cherry round the waist, dragged him away from her. Again his sword was used to grim effect, and Miles turned to deal with the last man. He was armed, and had his sword out immediately, releasing Cherry as he faced this unexpected attack.

Miles fenced cautiously. The passage was narrow, and the cobbles gave precarious footing. He soon found that his opponent was a skilled swordsman, and not to be vanquished readily. But he was obviously bothered at having his fellows overcome so easily, despite the surprise advantage Miles had had. Also, he was desperately anxious, it seemed, not to lose Cherry, for he kept trying to glance round to see what she was doing.

Miles, who was facing Cherry, for the man was between them, called to her to run, but she paid no heed, and waited watching the fight.

At length, Miles saw an opening and lunged. The man parried it, and attempted a riposte, but, using a daring stroke Miles twisted his wrist, and sent his opponent's sword clattering to the ground as he himself struck and pierced the man's shoulder, causing him to drop to the ground clasping it in agony. He was out of the fight, and Miles wasted no time on him, but sprang across his body towards Cherry.

'My dearest love! What are you doing

here? You run the risk of such attacks foolishly.'

He took her in his arms, and with a sob, she leant against him.

'Miles! Oh, Miles!'

For a few moments they were incapable of speech, then Miles recovered his wits.

'I will escort you home,' he said firmly. 'You shall not be subject to such attacks again. Why in heaven's name did you not bring a servant?'

'No!'

She had recovered, and stepped back. 'I have something I must do! They are going to arrest Harry, I must warn him.'

'Arrest?'

'Oh, please, forget what I have said, I am confused!'

She looked at him wildly, and he took her firmly in hs arms again.

'My beloved, you may warn your friend, but I am not allowing you to go home alone. Where does he live?'

She indicated the way, and he put his

arm comfortingly about her as they walked along. It was with a strange sense of unreality that he realised that she was taking him to Sir Henry Villiers' lodgings. As they reached the door, Cherry looked pleadingly at Miles.

'I promise I will not run away, but I must see Harry alone. Will you wait for me here?'

'I do not understand, but this Harry is Sir Henry Villiers, I take it?'

'Aye, do you know him?' she asked in surprise.

'Yes. I was on my way to visit him myself when I saw you.'

'But what, how?'

'That can wait. You have news that his arrest is planned? Is that it?'

'Yes, I must warn him. Those men were waiting to entrap me, they must have been warned. I must try to help Harry escape while there is time.'

Miles knocked on the door. 'I will wait here if you prefer it, but I also have dealings with Sir Henry. May I come with you?'

Too confused to resist, Cherry nodded, and Sir Henry's man opened the door to them at that moment.

'Is Sir Henry up yet?' Cherry asked urgently.

'No, Mistress, but I will tell him you are here. Good morning, Mr. Talbot.'

He showed them into a small parlour, and within a few minutes, during which time they had not spoken, Sir Henry joined them.

'Miles? Cherry? What is this?'

'Harry, you must go away immediately. There are plans to arrest Gerard and the others, and your name was mentioned. They have made another plot against Cromwell, and mean to kill him in chapel at Whitehall this morning, but they will be arrested first. I was set upon as I came here, and but for Mr. Talbot's intervention, they would have had me.'

'Who has betrayed us?'

'I know not, but they intend coming here. Go into the country for a while. I do not believe they have evidence against you, merely suspicion.'

Sir Henry nodded. 'I must go, it seems.'

'Is there aught I can do to help you? Are there papers to be burnt?' Miles asked.

'No, my friend. I do not keep incriminating papers about me. I am a lawyer, after all. All I need do is pack my bags and leave.'

'Leave your man to pack, and go at once,' Cherry urged. 'They are already on the move. Miles dealt with those three, but there will soon be others, and if they find you here, they will not let you go. Please, Harry, leave now. Come with us.'

'No, I would not incriminate you. They may have my name, but there is nought to connect either of you with me, unless these lodgings have been watched, and even then, your visits here are not proof of aught but social intercourse. Unless they know something else, you are both safe. I will leave as soon as I am dressed. You must go now.'

'He is right, Cherry. Good fortune, Sir Henry, and I will endeavour to contact you in a short while. I planned to go to the King, I will come into Norfolk when I return.'

'Farewell, my friends, we will soon be meeting again, I am certain.'

They left, after carefully making sure that there was no one watching the house. By now there were several people about the streets, and they were not conspicuous as they walked through the City.

Neither of them tried to talk. They were both busy working out the implications of what they had discovered about each other. Both were recalling the fears they had had that the other was trying to obtain information, and pondering this discovery that they appeared to be on the same side.

Cherry led the way through the lesser streets and alleys to the back of her house, where Miles had on the previous occasion watched her let herself unobtrusively into the house.

There was no one about, and Cherry slipped through the gate and across the yard to a small doorway which led into a passage beside the kitchen. Sounds of activity came from it, but no one was visible, and Cherry moved quietly along the passage to a narrow staircase. She ran lightly up this, and Miles followed. At the top she went through a small room that opened into her bedroom.

Reaching its safety, she turned and faced Miles, to be crushed to him in a breathtaking embrace. As he kissed her, he tasted the salt tears on her cheeks, and drew back in surprise.

'My sweet one, my love, what is't? There is no need to fear any more. You are safe.'

'No, that is not why I am being so stupid,' she said, brushing away the tears with her hand.

'Then what, my dear one?'

'I have been in such anguish,

thinking you did not love me!' she told him.

'Thinking I did not love you!' Miles stared at her. 'Was it not obvious that I could not bear to be apart from you?'

'I could not tell. Oh, yes, I knew you wanted my body, but that is not love. You said many fine words to me, but when you rescued me just now was the first time you called me your love!'

'I was afraid,' he said slowly. 'Afraid of coming too much under your spell, and I tried to fight against it.'

'As with me,' she whispered.

'There is so much to say, I know not where to begin!'

She laughed, a little tremulously.

'I know what I am going to do. I need to discard these wretched clothes, and then we will have breakfast. You will not object that it is not supper?' she said, a gleam of mischief in her eyes.

'Not in the least, my love. Supper comes afterwards, and the longer the wait, the longer the anticipation.'

'Fie on you. 'Tis Sunday morning,

too! What would the Puritans say to hear you?'

'I care nought for them, for the day, nor for the time,' he declared, attempting to take her into his arms again.

Laughingly she eluded him, and shook her fist chidingly.

'Pray await me in my boudoir, sir,' she murmured, and disappeared back into the room they had come through on the way from the back of the house.

Miles grinned, and resisted the temptation to follow her. Instead, he went through into the boudoir, and settled himself on a low couch to wait for her.

In a surprisingly short time she joined him, and was her usual neatly dressed and perfectly groomed self. She had put on a demure dove grey gown, trimmed with pink ribbons. The plainness of it merely accentuated her femininity, as it clung to the curves of her body. Miles could not look away as she approached him.

'Come, let us eat, and leave explanations until afterwards. Breakfast is already laid in the dining parlour, and I know not what you have been doing all night, but I have been working hard, and need it!'

So saying, she moved towards the door, and he sprang up to open it for her.

He was hungry and tired after his night of walking, and the exertion of the fight, and despite his anxiety to discover all about Cherry, he acquiesced in her wishes. They ate the meat and cheese provided, and the ale washed it down. They spoke very little, seeming content while they ate to gaze at one another, and commenting only briefly on the most trivial of things. When they had finished, and had recovered from the excitements of the early morning, they both felt readier to make the explanations that were called for.

'Shall we move to the boudoir if you have finished?' Cherry suggested at last.

Miles nodded, and she went before him.

Cherry seated herself in a chair by the window, and waved Miles to another, but he shook his head, and sat on the floor beside her, taking her hand in his.

'Shall I begin?' he asked.

11

'Please.' Cherry answered. 'Who are you? What are you?'

'I use my own name,' he began, smiling at her. 'My family have estates in Wiltshire. My brother, Sir Thomas is head of the family now, and I have two sisters. We are distant kin of the Earl of Shrewsbury.'

'I am glad that is your name,' she said musingly. 'I like 'Miles', and would find it difficult to get used to another. You are a soldier?'

'Yes. Much of what I told you was true, though I could not tell you that I had fought for the King. I was born the year Charles the first came to the throne, and as soon as I was eighteen I joined my father and brother in the army. I fought until the King was imprisoned in forty seven, but my father was killed at Marston Moor.'

'And 'twas then that you joined the Dutch?'

'Yes. My brother retired to the estates, and compounded in order not to lose them, but I went abroad and fought with the Dutch for a time.'

'Till Worcester?' she asked softly.

'Aye. I joined Charles as he marched south through England, having managed to cross to England as soon as it was certain he was making the invasion. 'Twas there I had the scar you were so concerned about,' he said, glancing up at her.

'Yes, and when you were rescued by a lady, I seem to recall,' she retorted.

He laughed. 'I must take you to meet Meg one day. She has a large and growing family, and her husband was my dear comrade in many battles.'

'How did she rescue you? I am intrigued.'

'I hid under her bed,' he answered, and laughed at the amused look in her eyes.

'Not in it, sir? How unlike you not to

take such an opportunity!'

'She was in the midst of labour, or that was what the roundheads thought when they came searching the house. She gave a most convincing display, and they could scarce leave the room fast enough. There was an old midwife from the village in the plot, and she was regaling them with the most fearsome stories of what would happen if they did not depart immediately. The birth of a monster through the fright my lady was suffering was the least of them. I could scarce control my laughter.'

Cherry laughed. 'You are fortunate in your lady friends,' she commented. 'How many more have protected you?'

'None so effectively as Meg.'

'And since then?'

'I have been working for the King, travelling round, meeting people who might be willing to help him back to his throne.'

'Why did you come to me?'

'I needed to get to know some of the Parliament men, and Robert Peyton suggested that I would meet such at your house.'

'So I was right! You did try to discover secrets from me.'

'Aye, to my shame. After I met you, I came to despise myself for treating you so, but my loyalty to the King came first. If 'tis any consolation, I learned nought from you!'

'No. I was careful, and on my guard, for I suspected you. But I was so terrified that I would say something, which is why I have been avoiding you!'

He kissed the hand he was fondling.

'What did you suspect me of?'

'I was afraid that you might be an agent of Thurloe's. They often try to discover who is reliable, and since so many Parliament men come here, they might well have been suspicious of me.'

'But all the time you were working for us. How does that happen?'

'I was brought up in Norfolk, which was strongly Parliamentarian. But I disliked the sobriety the Puritans demanded. Then, when I was but thirteen, I fell in love with a neighbour's son. Harry Villiers. We planned to marry. He was a few years older than I, and had a title, though he was not rich. I had a good dowry, we did not fear opposition. But Harry's family were Royalist, and my parents would not hear of the match. They had had an offer from a rich London merchant, and forced me into accepting him.'

'I cannot imagine your being forced into ought you found distasteful,' he said, curious.

'Can you not? I should mayhap have said tricked me. Harry was away, in the army, and they told me that he had been killed. I was so overborne with grief that I cared not what became of me, and agreed largely to escape from home. By the time I found that Harry was still alive, I had been hastily married off. I was but fourteen.'

Miles slipped his arm round her waist, and she leaned for a moment against him before continuing.

'Fortunately my husband did not

216

bother me overmuch after the first few weeks, but they were horrible enough. He was an impatient man, and I was very young and inexperienced. When he found me unsatisfactory, he turned to other woman, for which I was heartily thankful.'

'Did he illtreat you?'

'What have you heard?' she said, looking down at him sombrely. 'I cannot believe you have not discussed me?'

'Of course, a little. I heard that he beat you badly.'

'Yes, frequently, but that was his right. I dare say I was a great trial to him, for I would not do all he demanded. There were certain things he expected of me that I could not do.'

She shuddered, and Miles held her close. After a while, she went on.

'Once, I was so ill afterwards that my brother came and threatened to kill him unless he left me alone. After that, 'twas not so bad, and as he was away with the army, I did not have to suffer him for too much time. You can understand that when he was killed by the Royalists at Dunbar I was not sorry? 'Twas something to be grateful for. I was rich, still young, only twenty, and best of all, free. My father had died, and my mother was married again, so there was no one to order me about. My brother realised what I had been through, and wished only that I should enjoy life. It was while I was in Norfolk in seclusion after the death of Weston that I met Harry again.'

'He had not remained unwed?' Miles said, mentally recalling Sir Henry's rich wife and large family.

'No, and in many ways I was relieved, for he would most like have pressed me to marry him, and I had no wish for it. With him, for I did not love him any longer, or with anyone, for I wished to remain free.'

'How did he take your marriage?'

'Methinks he was glad, though he had been angry when he first heard about it. But soon he was offered an heiress, and he did not remember me long.'

She giggled suddenly. 'I do not think I could have put up with being left in the country, treated as a brood mare! Harry seems to have forgot our childhood love, for he is always so proud to tell me how many children his Emma has borne him! I think he might have displayed more tact, and at least pretended that he did not care for her!'

'But you do not care for him?'

'No, not one slight remnant of feeling remains, and I realised that when we met again, though I had often, before, thought nostalgically of him and wished that life had fallen out differently. Now, of course, I am glad, and can forget the bad time.'

'How did you meet?'

'Mayhap you heard of the Norfolk rising? In the winter after Dunbar. 'Twas centered on Downham, where a new fencing school was opened as cover for meetings. Then men began to attend hunting parties wearing swords. Really,' she laughed abruptly, 'these men have no more idea of how to conspire than children! They seemed to feel 'twas all a game!'

'I would exclude myself, naturally,' Miles laughed at her. 'But 'tis too true, unfortunately.'

'Oh, yes, I can tell that for you 'tis no game, 'tis all most serious, you never derive any pleasure out of it!'

He gently bit her fingers, and laughingly she rapped his head with her other hand. When he attempted to pull her down to the floor with him, she protested.

'No, no. I must finish telling you! Behave!'

'Well, finish, woman, and do not give way to your natural disgust at the inferiority of these men. You will learn that I am different!'

Ignoring this provoking remark, she continued.

'The plotters met towards the end of

November, but there were less than two hundred of them, and they were defeated without even fighting. Their moves had been known, and Rich with the county militia dispersed them. 'Twas pathetic!'

'Was Sir Henry involved?'

'Yes. He was fortunate because he escaped. About a quarter of them were taken prisoner, and half of those executed. If Harry had been taken he would have been executed, for he was one of the leaders, from what he told me. But he escaped, and came to me. I was staying at my old home, in supposed seclusion after my husband's death ten weeks or so before, and Harry did not dare to go home to his wife, for they were watching for him. He could not reach the coast, and he knew that our house had an old priest hole, for we had often explored it when we were very young children. I hid him there, and managed to distract the party that came to search.' She paused, staring silently before her. 'That was the beginning of it all.'

'Tell me,' he said quietly, holding her hand firmly.

''Twas Dick Ashford who came with a few men. He made it plain that he admired me, and since he was so determined to search the place minutely, and the old hiding place was not very well concealed, I had to distract him. He sent the men away, and that was that. When he left, he had not searched the house.'

'You were willing to do that for Sir Henry, whom you did not love?'

'I could not see him taken and killed. I had once loved him, and besides, he had a wife and babes depending on him.'

'Even so, he was fortunate, and you were courageous.'

Cherry laughed. 'Do not pity me too greatly! Dick is a handsome man, and I found it not so distasteful as I had expected. After all, the only other man I had known was my husband, and he was — brutal!'

'Not many women would have been so generous!'

'But I was baptised Charity! 'Twas about time I began to live up to the hopes my parents had for me!'

'I doubt they had such hopes,' Miles laughed.

Cherry shrugged. ''Twas then that the idea of helping the King came to me. Dick had been most talkative, and I had, without intending to, discovered much. He was most anxious to see me again and I agreed, saying that once my mourning was over I intended to return to London. I told him sufficient to make him sorry for me, and realised that he was not one of the killjoy Puritans. I could use him to get to know the other Parliament men, and learn much. The only difficulty was that I knew no one to pass on any information I obtained.'

'That was where Sir Henry came in?'

'Yes. I had discovered where they meant to search next, and I was able to tell him, and save some of the other men, but of course he guessed how I had obtained the information. I told him my plans, and he at first tried to dissuade me.'

'I am glad of that, at least. It shows some proper feeling in him.'

'But I would not be dissuaded. In the end he said that he had himself been approached to act as a means of collecting information in London. He was hesitating, but I managed to persuade him to do the job, and I think he did not wish to appear to be outdone by a woman. So I had my source of information, and my method of passing it on.'

'I wonder how you persuaded him?' Miles said musingly.

Cherry tweaked his ear. 'Not how you think! Harry would no sooner think of going to bed with me than he would join the New Model Army! He is a faithful husband!'

'And so you began this life?'

'Yes. I had many acquaintances, and was rich enough to entertain lavishly. I knew that Dick would protect me against accusations of the Puritans, and dared to give parties. My friends were so pleased to come that they soon gained a reputation, and many more people began to attend. Dick brought his friends, and I was able to discover a great deal about Army matters from him. Then I came to know John Taunton, and he is as indiscreet as Dick, but as he works for Thurloe, that is most useful I have been able to give warning of many arrests in that way.'

'And you thought I was worth trying?' he asked.

'No. At least, I did not know who or what you were, and I confess I tried to find out. But I had asked you to stay because I could not help myself! Please believe that!'

'My dearest one! I too felt the same.'

'I did not discover aught, and thought in fact that you were trying to use me, or trap me. I tried to stop seeing you, but I could not. These last few times, I have so longed to ask you to stay with me, instead of John, but he was providing me with vital information about Gerard and I dared not lose the opportunity with things so desperate!'

'My poor beloved! Have you not hated having to use your body in this way?'

'Not until I met you. I had been sold to my husband, and in truth it seemed but the same. At least 'twas more pleasant! But after I knew you, I hated every minute of it!'

'Then you do love me, my dearest one?'

She looked down at him, her face serious. 'I do. I did not understand at first why my life, which had seemed so satisfactory with my work so important, should suddenly become tawdry. When first I saw you you reminded me of Harry, though you are not alike in features. I did not understand why, until I realised that he was the only man I have ever loved, and you inspired the same feeling in me, though,' she hastened to add, 'with you 'tis so very much stronger.'

'Cherry, my dearest, I love you so. Let me take you to Flanders and you can wait for me there.'

She looked at him in surprise. 'To Flanders? Why? Do you intend to leave England?'

'No, I have work still to do. But you are endangered, you must leave.'

'I am not in danger, I am certain. I discovered that Harry and Gerard and some others were to be arrested, but there is nought to connect me with Harry. I always wear those dreadful clothes when I go to him, and would seem some inferior maid servant.'

''Tis no disguise. I recognised you once before, and followed you, for I could not think what my charmingly elegant hostess did in such clothes. Then, of course, I did not know Sir Henry, otherwise we might have been spared much pain and suspicion of one another.'

'I still do not think I have aught to fear, and besides, I have Dick and John as protectors, they would not allow me to be taken.'

'They might not be able to prevent it.'

'I am in no danger, truly,' she insisted.

'What of the men who were trying to arrest you this morning?'

'They were merely taking anyone who approached Harry's house. We were almost at the door, and there are scarcely any other doors in that courtyard. They must have been stopping everyone on suspicion. Especially at that hour. I am certain they did not know who I was. I knew none of them.'

'I do not like it,' he persisted.

'But I still have work to do.'

'No!' he said vehemently.

'What do you mean?'

'I will not have you sell yourself to men in such a fashion.'

'I do not like it,' she said gently. 'I never have, though it has not been as bad as my marriage was. I should not have said that I hated it. You must hate many of the things you are forced to do. But 'tis a weapon I can use, and 'tis still there for use. Would you have me desert the King's cause merely because I have met you and fallen in love with you? You have not suggested giving up your work, in fact you say you cannot.'

'This is different,' he said firmly. 'I am going to marry you, and I will not have my wife used so!'

'You have forgotten something,' she said quietly.

It was his turn to look surprised. 'What do you mean?'

'You have not asked me to marry you, and you cannot force me to do so.'

He stared at her in dismay. 'My love! You are not going to refuse?'

She rubbed her eyes, a gesture of weariness that smote him with compassion for her.

'I should not ask you! My beloved, you are tired, you have been awake all night, and 'tis mid morning now. You need to sleep.'

He stood up, and pulled her out of the chair.

'When you have slept, we will talk further. Would you like me to go away and return later this evening?'

She smiled at him. 'I love you so dearly,' she whispered. 'Stay with me. I feel so wonderfully safe in your arms.'

He lifted her and carried her through to the bedroom, and there gently helped her out of her gown. She sighed with pleasure as the cool sheets touched her body, and soon he slipped in beside her, and cradled her to him. Already she was almost asleep, and roused herself to murmur his name. He looked down at her and determined fiercely that she would never belong to any other man in the future. Then he too, exhausted by the events of the night, slept.

12

It was almost dusk before Miles stirred. He woke slowly, wondering for a moment where he was. Then he realised that Cherry was lying beside him, his arm still around her, and the events of the previous night came back to him. He lay watching Cherry, considering all she had told him of her former life, and surmising the parts she had glossed over. A wave of anger swept over him as he thought of James Weston ill-treating and abusing her, and for a moment he wished that he had the man before him so that he could choke the life out of him. Realising the absurdity of that, he smiled ruefully at himself.

He began to consider what he was to do. He could not bear the idea of Cherry continuing with the life she had been leading, but he thought she might feel bound to carry on with it while it was of use. Should he try to insist, or should he acquiesce? For a wild moment he thought of giving up his own work, and suggesting that they settle safely and peacefully in the country, but knew that they would both despise that way out. He had not resolved the puzzle before Cherry woke. She stretched, and her supple limbs touched his, awakening desire in him.

Feeling him, she opened her eyes, and immediately recalled events. She rolled over towards him and smiled.

'Thank you, my dear. I hope you slept well, for I did, and feel refreshed.'

He kissed her, and she returned the kiss passionately.

'I suppose you have work to do, and I have been distracting you from it,' she said, lacing her fingers behind his head.

'Indeed I have work to do, but you have been no distraction apart from the fact that you have been asleep.'

'What is it?' she asked, pulling his

head towards her so that she could kiss him.

'I have to make you love me so much that you can never bear to consider parting from me,' he assured her, half seriously.

She laughed. 'I can tell you now that 'tis a task you have succeeded in. There is no need for further effort on your part, my dearest love.'

'Nevertheless, I intend to make the effort,' he retorted, and did so, thoroughly and effectively, prolonging the moments of ecstacy with all the skill at his command, so that Cherry was loved as she had never been loved before, for all her experience.

When at last they were satisfied, they lay in each others arms, and talked and talked. They spoke much more of their earlier lives, and for some time did not broach the topic of the future. It was by now dark, and they had not lit the candle beside the bed, but after some time, Cherry sat up and felt for the tinderbox.

'I am hungry,' she declared. 'I trust my servants have prepared supper. I am sorry that you have missed your dinner.'

'What excellent servants you have, my dear, to leave you in peace and to prepare meals for you and your guests without needing to be supervised.'

'I pay them well, and treat them fairly. They know my erratic ways. If I miss a meal, or sleep during the day and not at night, that is my affair, and they do not question it. They merely carry on and are prepared for whatever I request of them.'

'Still admirable. I wish we had you at the head of our Sealed Knot. You would organise affairs so much better than they do!'

Cherry laughed. 'Then, I suppose, you would have me mounted on a charger, leading the cavalry in the decisive battle that is to restore the King?'

'You would decimate the enemy by merely looking at them.'

'Oh, come, I am no Medusa!'

'No, I did not mean that,' Miles protested, laughing as she tried to pull his hair. 'I meant that they would be so overcome by your beauty that they would refuse to fight you.'

'Then I wish I had the same effect on you,' she panted, as she struggled to free her hands that he grasped firmly.

'Ah, but they do not know you and your deceitful ways as I do.'

'What have you in mind for me afterwards? Marriage to the King, who would henceforth be content to allow me to rule his country?'

'That reminds me, I must not allow Charles Stuart to meet you. If I do, you will forget me instantly, and fall under his charm.'

'What, do you admit that he has more than you?' she asked in mock surprise.

'No, by no means, but the novelty, added to the glamour of a crown, even though he does not yet wear it, might overwhelm you.'

'Methinks you are more like to do

that, Miles Talbot!' she retorted. 'Now, do you mean to keep me prisoner all night, fainting for lack of food?'

He laughed and released her, and they slipped on loose robes and went through to the dining parlour, where a delectable supper had been laid out for them.

As the meal progressed, they returned to seriousness.

'You mentioned to Harry that you planned to visit the King. When do you plan to go?'

'I was intending leaving within a day or so.'

'Will you be gone long?'

'I do not know. I wish to present to the King the desires of many of his supporters for more action, for a livelier group of leaders than those of the Sealed Knot. 'Tis dissatisfaction with them that causes wild plots like Gerard's to be concocted.'

'They will have been arrested by now,' Cherry said suddenly. 'While we were sporting and sleeping, they will have been arrested. I should have attempted to reach them, as well as Harry.'

'No, you should not, for you could have done no good. I attempted to dissuade Gerald to abandon the original plan, but he would neither listen to reason, nor accept my warnings that the plot was known. He would not have listened to you and he must pay for his folly.'

'I wonder how many have been taken? I did not discover all the names of those they suspected.'

'Cherry, you are in danger, come with me,' Miles urged suddenly. ''Tis bound to be discovered sooner or later that you have been spying on them.'

'I am prepared for that,' she said quietly. 'But until it is discovered, I can be of use.'

'Then you will not give it up and marry me while there is time for you to escape?'

'Miles, you torment me! I desire nought so much as to be rid of it all, with the deceits and the problems, yes, and the danger, and to be always with you. Yet you will not give up your task because of the danger. Why ask it of me?'

He regarded her for a long time. 'No, you are right, 'tis simply that I cannot bear to let another man touch you!'

She closed her eyes, and breathed deeply. 'I do not think I could bear it myself,' she said slowly. 'This morning, I thought that I could steel myself to do it, but you did more successful work this last hour than you know!'

'Then, what holds you back?'

'I think that I can still, simply by seeing these men, learn things of value. I will make excuses, and 'twill serve for a time, they will not be suspicious. They are so accustomed to confiding in me that they may still do so, without the seductions of the past.'

'They will not listen for long to your excuses. Not if they are as full blooded as I take them to be.'

'I will contrive.'

He sat silently for a while, and then looked across at her.

'Why should we not marry and live here? I have been thinking 'twould be necessary to take you away, and to break with your old friends, and wed in secret, but why need we do that?'

She looked at him, startled, but immediately began to consider this new idea.

'And we could both be working for the King, yet I have both the perfect excuse for dismissing them from my bed, and you as well! Miles, I believe it might serve! Yet, we double the risk to each other.'

'No, not if we are cautious. They must know that I have been attracted to you, and have probably been as jealous of me as I have been of them. Have neither Dick nor John asked you to marry them?'

She laughed. 'No, indeed, for they are both already married. That has been to some extent my protection. They cannot insist on staying with me too often, and become possessive, nor can they object if I take other lovers. And they would be in severe trouble with their wives and with their superiors if 'twere discovered that they spent time so with me! They cannot betray me without making far greater trouble for themselves.'

'Then as far as they are concerned, 'twould be natural for you to take a husband. You can still entertain, and hope to learn something, and at the very least maintain their friendship, which has its uses.'

'Miles, I begin to hope!'

'I see no real objection. Of course, 'twill be said that I cannot do my work so well, and I fear that may be true, but neither can I concentrate on it while I am in such uncertainty about you! I fear though, that if I am discovered, you will be endangered.'

'That would be no more than the risk I run already. But if John remains our friend, he might warn us. He would hear of moves against you, for he is high in Thurloe's confidence.'

'I do not think much of Thurloe's choice, if his lieutenants are so careless as John Taunton,' Miles said consideringly.

'You are decrying my powers!' she said, pouting and trying not to laugh.

'Merely comparing them with mine. After all, you confessed you learned nought from me!'

'Not immediately, but I know far more now than I know about John. What if I were acting, and mean to betray you now?'

'When will you marry me? Tomorrow?' he responded to this suggestion.

'I cannot! 'Twould seem too sudden to be convincing. I have had to pay a great deal of attention to John the last few weeks, while this plot was in the air. I cannot abruptly marry another man. Pay your visit to the King, and I will prepare the way here, and wed you as soon as you return. That will appear better.'

''Twill be just as sudden then,' he pointed out.

'No, for I will have realised during your absence that you mean a great deal to me, and when you return I will be swept off my feet! How is that?'

'I wish that there were playhouses, and that women played parts as in France,' he murmured, and she laughed, and threw a manchet of bread at him.

'Do you accept my conditions, sir? Marriage when you return, or not at all.'

'Then so be it. I am sure there are many risks we have not considered, but I do not care for them now I have you for my own.'

They soon returned to bed, and Miles did not leave until the next morning. He had decided to postpone his departure for the continent until certain news of the arrests had been received, and they expected that it would take a day or so to become known.

When the news was learned, it was far more serious than Miles had anticipated. Besides the Gerard plotters, six in all, who had been arrested that Sunday morning, Sir Richard Willys had been taken, and Lord Belasyse was in a state swaying between anger and fear when Miles saw him.

'I am told that he thinks I betrayed him,' he spluttered. ''Tis preposterous! The man is demented! But 'tis not safe to stay in London, while he is held he may think to save his own wretched skin by betraying us. I have told the rest of the Knot to disperse, and I am off myself within the hour.'

'You mean to break off all plans?' Miles asked in dismay.

'Not so, not so, my boy. We will continue with our work, naturally, but in a safer place, and at a safer time, when the clamour over this business has died down.'

'I see,' Miles said, realising that to argue would be pointless, for the man was thoroughly unnerved.

'We can do little else,' Lord Belasyse said petulantly, realising that he was making a poor showing. 'We have been attempting to discourage such hotheads as the faction round Lord Gerard, but they were determined to try and wrest the leadership of the Royalists here in England from the Knot. They are encouraged by Rupert's Swordsmen, and unless the King can give us more authority, we can do little else.'

'It can only leave the field clear for others if the Knot disperses,' Miles pointed out.

'We do not intend to give up completely,' Lord Belasyse said stiffly. 'Now, if you will excuse me, I must finish some letters before I go.'

Miles left him to it, and returned to his own lodgings, more disturbed then ever at the way things were going. The men of the Knot were showing themselves incapable of real leadership in the difficult conditions of the time. He did not see hotheads like Lord Gerard and his cousin John as leaders, even were they not now betrayed. He began to consider other Royalists amongst those he had talked with, and slowly a list of possible alternatives to the Knot formed in his mind. He must do his utmost to persuade the King to use some of them, and try thus to restore Royalist confidence in England.

During the next few days, more of the Gerard conspirators were rounded up, and there was news of more arrests in the country areas. When Miles spoke of these to Cherry, she told him some disturbing suspicions that had been aroused in her.

'John was with me last night,' she said slowly, then hastily added 'just for supper, you understand, I made an excuse to send him away. He was jubilant over the arrests. When I praised him and the Secretary for obtaining so many names, he said that Cotes had done his work well. I asked if Cotes was a fellow agent, implying that he had been clever, and John said that he had somewhat different tasks. He would not tell me more, and I dared not press it. But it seems strange that Thurloe knew so many and was able to swoop so effectively at just the right time.'

'You suggest that Cotes, whoever he is, might not simply have been in the councils of the plotters, but something else?'

'John was positive that he was no ordinary agent, that he had other tasks. I have puzzled and puzzled over it, and I suddenly recalled the name being mentioned once before. 'Twas last October or November, as far as I can recall, and John was talking with a friend he sometimes brings here, one I suspect of being an agent. I overhead a few words, and they sounded so nonsensical they stayed in my mind. He said, 'With Cotes and his spurs, he will uncover when the time is ripe.' I thought he was talking of clothes, but 'twas not that, but the name Cotes.'

'And the spurs could have been encouragements, and the uncovering a betrayal?' Miles said slowly. 'Then, it makes sense. You think this Cotes was trepanning Gerard?'

'I can think of no other explanation. If Thurloe gets his spies to infiltrate an organisation, why should they not lead the others on to commit more follies, and provide causes for arrest? Then he would be able to trace the most likely rebels.'

'Aye. And so often men have been arrested and then quickly released. If the experience does not prevent them from plotting again, they can always be taken again on suspicion, or when some rising is expected, to circumvent them or frighten others. This has happened to many I could name.'

'We must discover who he is, and warn our friends.'

'Or quietly dispose of him,' Miles said thoughtfully.

'Is it not better to know who is working against us? If he were gone there could be someone else, and probably unsuspected. Better to know the traitors.'

'There is some merit in that,' Miles agreed, 'but we cannot warn everyone he might contact, and 'twould take time to place another man who would be accepted. No, I think we must try to render him harmless.'

'Then while you are away I will endeavour to find out more about him.'

'Will John not be curious if you question him?'

'I was not planning to question John. No, Harry was in contact with many plotters, though Gerard never, as far as I know, was in touch with him. But he may know something, at least names of people involved that I can follow up.'

'Do not write, the post is too dangerous. Can you trust one of your excellent servants with a message?'

'Not so complicated a one. I will have to go to Norfolk, to deal with business there. 'Twill not be thought strange, I often go for a few days, usually when I need peace from my life here. At least there I shall be free from the attentions of John and Dick,' she finished lightly, touching his hand as it lay on the table between them.

'Is that a lure to induce me to agree?' he asked, holding her hand tightly.

'No, for I do not need to use such devices with you. We are so much in accord.'

'When will you go?' Miles asked.

'As soon as I can rearrange my engagements here. I have parties planned for next week, but I can tell everyone then that I shall be away. I can leave at the end of the week. When are you going?'

'I must go tomorrow,' Miles told her abruptly, and she gave a cry of dismay. 'I have been putting it off, but I must do so no longer. I could not bear to tell you before, and I did not wish to make more of our meetings sad than I had to. I am too cowardly.'

'No, my love, not that! I have known that we must part soon, and must face it. Besides, the sooner you go, the sooner we can marry when you come back.'

They made the most of their last few hours together, and then Miles dragged himself away, much earlier than usual, for he had many things to attend to before he left on his journey. It was this earlier departure that enabled the two bullies hired by Faithful Denham to watch the house to follow him.

They had been employed by the furious little man for six months, and even he was beginning to get tired of the whole affair, but a certain vindictive stubbornness made him continue to pay them in return for a report each week of who stayed late at Cherry's house.

They had watched Dick Ashford and John Taunton many times, and much as it caused Faithful to writhe at the thought of them enjoying Cherry's favours, he was powerless to harm them. Dick was on friendly terms with the Protector, and Faithful dare not accuse him. John was one of Thurloe's most valued spies, and similarly would be protected from Faithful by his master. Faithful had considered simply causing them to be attacked as they made their way home in the darkness, but much as he felt that would be a suitable punishment for them, he knew that it would not satisfy him. He needed to gloat over his victim, and stress the fact that he had been instrumental in bringing him to ruin.

He maintained the watch because he could not forget the man he had himself followed and lost the bitterly cold December night. He was convinced that it had been neither Ashford nor Taunton, and the thought of yet another man as a lover of Cherry made him at the same time furiously angry, and hopeful that here might be someone less powerfully protected on whom he could take his revenge.

Miles had previously escaped their vigilance because he had stayed so long with Cherry. Unlike Ashford and Taunton, who had wives to check on their absences, he had been able to stay whole nights, and usually left only at dawn. The watchers had by then given up, not wishing to be seen at their post by the servants as they began the day's work. But this night he was unfortunate, and realising that this might at last be the man Faithful had long insisted was another visitor, they were careful to follow as closely as possible.

Miles was thoughtful as he walked along, and though he kept the usual wary eye for footpads, and his hand on his sword, he was careless and did not realise that he was being followed. He was regretting his parting with Cherry, made possible only by the thought that the unbelievable had happened, and he was to marry her. Then, reluctantly, he began to think of the mission before him, and review the arguments he must use with the King.

Reaching his lodgings, he immediately began to pack, and then, with all in readiness, lay down for a couple of hours sleep before he set off. The men who had followed him settled down to wait until daybreak, and then, as the servants began to stir, they kept careful watch on the house where Miles stayed. They were fortunate, for very soon a maidservant came out swinging a pail and went to buy milk. She was a flirtatious piece, and one of the men was soon able to get into conversation with her, and learn Miles' name. Their work completed, they hurried to Faithful's house and delivered their report.

13

Faithful listened intently to the men, scarcely able to conceal his glee. He had sometimes wondered whether Miles was the man he sought, but had not been able to discover, from his jealous observation of them together, whether they were conducting a liaison. He had instinctively taken a dislike to Miles on sight, for he distrusted anyone young and handsome, tall and well built as Miles was. This was largely because he could not prevent his thoughts turning to the licentious pleasures he imagined them to indulge in. He was tormented by his imaginings, and even his fierce denunciations of such activities gave no relief to his twisted soul.

When the men had finished, he congratulated them, and bade them keep close watch for the next few nights. When they had gone, he rubbed his hands in delighted anticipation. He would denounce Miles, and have him imprisoned. He then realised that in order to do this, he would need to denounce Cherry also, and this gave him pause. He considered his moves carefully. Could he implicate Miles alone? He came to the conclusion that this would be impossible, and if he charged some other woman, it could easily be proved wrong. He was sitting anxiously scratching his head when there was a knock at the door.

Angrily he called on his servant to enter and demanded why he was to be disturbed.

'I beg pardon, Master, but you said that you wanted to be told at once if we caught the woman.'

'Eh? What woman? What are you babbling about, man?'

'The woman Tapsell, Mr. Denham. You remember, she was seen taking food from the kitchen, but we could not catch her.'

Faithful had managed to bring his

attention to the man.

'Aye, I remember. One of those disreputable beggars, wasn't she, always hanging round the doors. Where is she?'

'She is locked in the stable. we saw her passing by in the alley behind the house, and chased her.'

Faithful pondered, and then, an idea striking him, smiled in satisfaction.

'Bring her here,' he ordered.

'Here?' asked the servant in surprise.

'Aye!' his master snapped. 'And hasten!'

The servant obeyed quickly, for Mr. Denham was a bad man to cross. Within a very short time he was dragging into the parlour a skinny, frightened girl of little more than fourteen.

'Leave her, but wait outside the door.'

When they were alone, Faithful surveyed the girl. Under the grime and rags he detected a face that would be pretty if it were clean, and a figure that was just blossoming into maturity.

'I am going to give you over to the Justice for your thefts from me,' he said sternly.

The girl threw herself at his feet. 'No! Please, my lord, I ain't stole nought from you.'

'I have a ring, a gold ring missing. You stole it.'

'I did not! I swear it! Only a crust of bread, 'cause I was starving!'

'Then you admit it? If a crust of bread, why not the other?'

'What would I do with a gold ring?'

'Sell it, most like. I do not care. But you will be fortunate to escape with your life, and most like be sent to the colonies.'

She began to protest her innocence, and beg him to have pity on her, but he went on, remorselessly.

'Do you know what 'tis like there? Most people die of plague or fever, or are killed by the wild animals that roam freely all over the land.'

She was terrified by this, for she had seen bears and bulls being baited by dogs, and imagined these huge creatures surrounding her.

'Please, my lord, have pity!' she wailed.

'Mayhap, if you helped me, I could save you,' he went on, so quietly that it was some time before his meaning sank into her bemused brain.

She looked up. 'I'd do whatever you said, I would,' she sobbed, and he smiled in satisfaction. These people were so easy to gull!

' 'Twill mean a few weeks in prison, but I will give you some fine clothes and some money to make your stay as comfortable as possible,' he told her, and she scarcely hesitated. She had seen the inside of Newgate before, and it held few terrors for her.

'What must I do?' she whispered, almost eagerly.

'When you look more the part, after a bath and with decent clothes,' he began, but the mention of a bath had frightened the girl almost as much as the idea of deportation.

Faithful was impatient, and roughly told her to cease her noise, or he would simply hand her over now. She considered the alternatives, and, shuddering, decided that she must undergo the unknown terrors of a bath. She nodded, and he continued.

'When you look the part, I need you to swear before a Magistrate that you have had carnal relations with a certain man. I will tell you more about him later. Do you understand?'

She nodded. This was not so bad as she thought.

'Where is the man? When do you want me to bitch him?'

Faithful frowned. 'You do not have to do that,' he said, wrinkling up his nose. 'Just to say that you have.'

She shrugged. She did not understand, but what did it matter to her if she escaped the threat of deportation?

Faithful called to his servant, and told him to fetch Mistress Gadge, his housekeeper. When this redoubtable dame arrived, he handed the girl over to her, explaining that he wanted her to be made to look respectable, and given some clean clothes.

Mistress Gadge nodded, uncaring enough to ask why she was given these odd commands, and seized the girl with cruel fingers biting into her thin arm.

Faithful waited impatiently, and then, when the girl was brought back to him, surveyed her carefully. She was indeed pretty, in a pert way, and he thought that her story would be believed. He spent some time coaching her as to what she was to say, and then, satisfied, set off for the nearest Magistrate.

There, he explained that the girl had come to him to confess her wickedness, and beg for help to escape the sinful demands of a Mr. Miles Talbot. The Magistrate, who disliked Faithful, did not relish the task laid upon him, but there was little he could do for the girl maintained her story that this Mr. Talbot had accosted her one night, and debauched her, and had often since forced his attentions on her when he had met her unprotected in the streets.

'The villain has on more than one occasion forced his way into her room at night,' Faithful interposed.

'I will send to arrest him,' the Magistrate said at length, and Faithful, satisfied, promised to look after the girl until she should be required.

The following day, Faithful called to see whether Miles had been arrested, only to be told by a satisfied looking Magistrate that Mr. Talbot had left his lodgings early the previous morning, and his landlady did not know when he was expected to return, or where he had gone.

'What! He has flown! Did you give him warning?'

'Mr. Denham, I resent that, indeed I do!'

Faithful was too agitated to care, and rushed out of the room, leaving the Magistrate to ponder on these strange events.

Livid with fury, Faithful almost ran to the house Miles had lodged in, and demanded to see the landlady.

She, resenting his tone, was unforth-coming about her lodger, and refused indignantly when Faithful demanded to be shown the room.

'Indeed no, for he has paid me to retain it!'

'When is he coming back?'

'I know not,' she answered shortly, and Faithful could learn nothing from her.

Eventually he left, but he had barely stepped out of the house when he heard a girl's voice call after him.

Turning, he beheld a young maid-servant.

'You were asking about Mr. Talbot?' she said, looking round cautiously.

'Why? Do you know aught.'

'I might,' she said consideringly, and Faithful, sighing, jingled some coins in his pocket. Encouraged, the girl smiled. 'He was a fine looking man,' she said.

'Is that all you have to tell me?'

'Oh, no.' She paused, and Faithful almost shook her in his anxiety.

'Where has he gone?'

'Oh, I know nought about that, but I can tell you why he has gone.

'Then do so, girl!'

She smirked. 'He mentioned that he was getting wed. I expect he has gone to his home in the country to prepare it for his bride.'

Startled by the horrid suspicion that flashed into his mind, Faithful turned abruptly, and walked off, ignoring the indignant protests of the girl, who received no coins for her information. After pursuing him for a few yards, she called some rude words after him which he did not hear, and then flounced back into the house, resolving to exact payment first the next time she had anything to sell.

Faithful walked slowly home, twisting his hands together in agony. Was it true? Was that man going to wed Cherry? Fierce jealousy welled up in him, and he could scarcely walk, he was shaking with a mixture of anger and frustration. He sat at home in his parlour for hours, considering the situation, but doing little more than torture himself with mental pictures of Miles and Cherry making love.

Much later, he roused himself on recalling that Cherry had a party arranged for that night, and feverishly he made preparations, and went to her house.

He sat the whole evening in silence, but people were so accustomed to his sullen moods that no one took any notice of him. He was able to twist the knife in his wound when he heard Cherry explaining that she was soon visiting the country, setting off on the following Friday. This merely confirmed for Faithful that what he had surmised was true, and he went home in deep agony of mind, and sat the whole night in his chair, tormenting himself.

Miles had, unknowingly, escaped the net when he left early that morning, and his journey to Mons, where the King was staying at that time, was uneventful. He greeted Miles cheerfully, and begged to be told all that Miles knew of events.

Much of what Miles said about the events in England Charles already knew, but he was pleased to have Miles' opinions on them, for he rated him very highly as an agent and a judge of men. Miles explained the possibility of the Gerard faction being infiltrated by an agent provocateur, and Charles agreed that it seemed probable.

'We hope to discover who it is, Sire. We have some lead, the name Cotes. Have you any knowledge of such a person?'

'No, I cannot recall, but I will have enquiries made and inform you if I hear of aught. We must discover him.'

Miles went on to describe the sense of frustration he had found at the lack of activity and true leadership from the Sealed Knot. He stressed that this could lead to other mad plots like those of Gerard, and begged the King to sanction some other leaders.

Charles was thoughtful. 'I have received other similar representations,' he said. 'You advise it too?'

'Yes, I do, Sire. At first I was of the opinion that the direction had best be kept in the hands of a few people, the Knot, but I realise that they are not the ones likely to dare much in your cause. Others, many who have attempted to raise support for you in the past, might succeed in organising a rising. At the moment I see that as the best hope, for Cromwell is becoming stronger. There are even suggestions that he take the crown, and once that happened, 'twould be more difficult to dislodge him.'

'I will consider carefully, but before you go, have you any names of likely leaders?'

'Some that I have met, or that I know by repute. Sir Philip Musgrave, Sir Thomas Peyton, Sir Humphrey Bennett, Lord Byron. Many others, I will write them all down now I am safely here. But I beg that we contrive to use the Presbyterians. We cannot rely solely on the old Royalists. Many Presbyterians support you, even, I hear it rumoured, Fairfax himself. He has kept very quiet these last few years. I do not think he approved of his former lieutenant taking so much power to himself.'

Charles did not reply, but Miles was satisfied that he would consider the suggestion, and was pleased at the indication that the King was receiving similar advice from others besides himself. He spent a few more days at Mons, and had several more interviews with the King, then, with instructions to sound the people he had not yet seen, but thought might be useful, he returned to England.

Faithful had not awaited his return. For some days he had been in a stupor, unable to see to his business and incapable of any thought but of Cherry. He attended her last party, and though he was conscious of little else, absorbed the fact that she was leaving two days later early in the morning. This was a gay party, and Faithful stayed until the end, when he was firmly eased on his way by Dick Ashford. Jealously, Faithful watched John Taunton leave, and his mind began to function again as he wondered whether he or Dick would be creeping back to enjoy a last night in Cherry's arms.

Again he sat up all night, but by the morning the beginnings of a plan were working in his fevered brain. He sat before the fire he had ordered to be lit, despite the warm July day, and rocked back and forth as he worked out the details. Then he went to work, and spent what was left of the day visiting various people. At length, satisfied that he had done all that was necessary, he returned home smiling once more. For the first time since he had realised that Cherry was probably about to marry Miles, he sat and rubbed his hands together, and enjoyed a meal before falling exhausted into bed.

Cherry had been busy with her

packing and with plans for the changes she wished to make when Miles returned and they were married. She was making a last tour of the house with her housekeeper, giving last minute instructions before retiring to bed, when there was a knock on the door. She looked up, surprised, for it was late. The manservant who answered the door came to tell her that two men requested her presence, and she went to see who had sent this odd message.

In the parlour where the visitors had been shown, she found a Sergeant and a trooper of the Army.

'Well, gentlemen, what can I do for you?' she asked, puzzled.

They looked embarrassed, and the trooper began to straighten his already immaculate uniform.

The Sergeant coughed, and muttered something.

'Will you not sit down? Would you care for some wine?' Cherry asked, moving to where a decanter and glasses stood on a table.

'No, Mistress, I thank you,' the Sergeant said, and Cherry smiled, relieved to hear intelligible speech from him.

'Then will you not tell me why you are here? I was about to go to bed, for I start tomorrow on a journey.'

'Oh, no. That is, I am afraid you will be unable to go!' the man said abruptly, and Cherry stared at him in amazement.

'Not be able to go?' she repeated slowly. 'Why? What do you mean?'

'I very much regret it, Mistress. Please understand that I do but obey orders, I would not desire this, but I am under orders.'

Cherry found it increasingly difficult to keep her patience with the man, and spoke sharply.

'Pray be good enough to come to the point. What are you trying to tell me?'

He gulped. 'We have a warrant for your arrest.'

Cherry paled, and stepped back, feeling for a chair. The trooper, thinking that she was about to faint, stepped forward, but before he could reach her she had seated herself in the chair. She surveyed them calmly.

'I do not understand. Please explain.'

The Sergeant was full of further apologies, but she cut him short.

'On what charge am I arrested, and by whose instigation?'

The Sergeant looked at her unhappily. 'I know not how it started, Mistress, but the charge is twofold, for you are charged with adultery and fornication.'

Cherry almost laughed in relief. She had feared to hear charges of spying or activities against the state, and this, serious though it was, came as an anticlimax. She wondered briefly who was responsible, and then began to consider who would be most likely to be able to help her out of this entanglement.

'Then I suppose I must come with you, gentlemen. May I give some instructions to my staff first? As I told you, I was about to make a journey, and I must cancel my instructions regarding that.'

Relieved that she was taking it so calmly they made no demur, and she was able to give detailed instructions to her housekeeper, and also ask the woman to let Mr. Ashford know what had become of her.

'Tell him I depend on him,' she said firmly, and, having finished, turned to accompany her visitors.

'I am ready,' she said quietly. 'I do not propose to take much baggage, for 'tis all some stupid mistake, and I do not expect to be detained for long. My housekeeper will bring what I need most in the morning.'

'Ludgate, Mistress,' the Sergeant said briefly, and that was where Cherry was taken.

14

To Cherry's secret relief she was lodged in a room in the governor's house instead of in the cells. She was told that it had been paid for, and that she would be receiving a visitor tomorrow, but the Governor refused to say who that would be. She tried to compose herself to sleep, but could do little other than think of Miles, and wonder how this turn of events might affect them. She had little fear for herself, since she was confident that Dick or John would intervene to save her, if only in consideration of their own possible involvement. She was prepared to send to Elizabeth, Cromwell's daughter, if necessary, and ask her to intercede with her father, and she was certain that he would be able to refuse this beloved daughter nothing.

It was late the following morning

when Cherry's visitor was announced. She looked up, curious to see who this was, for she had been unable to determine who could know of her plight and be paying to provide her with superior accommodation. When Faithful Denham sidled into the room, she narrowed her eyes in sudden comprehension.

She had noticed his gloom on the two occasions he had been at her house the previous week, and, since she was skilled at estimating people's moods, she had realised that something more than his usual misery was affecting him. She had endeavoured to brighten him on the first evening, but had failed so signally that she had not even attempted more than casual conversation on the second evening.

Now, as she waited for him to cross the room towards her, she wondered just how much he knew. She had realised on first seeing him that she had him to thank for her arrest, but could not discern his motive.

'Mr. Denham!' she said in assumed surprise. 'What do you here?'

He came and looked at her in silence. She stared back, determined not to speak again until she could see what he intended.

'Do you not repent of your sinfulness?' he demanded suddenly, and she raised her eyebrows.

'Why, my friend, of what do you accuse me? Sinfulness? I beg of you, explain!'

'Do not attempt to fool me, as you have so many others! You are a whore, and a wanton hussy, and godly people should not be contaminated by you.'

Cherry stood up haughtily. 'Mr. Denham, if all you can do is abuse me in that fashion, I beg you to leave!'

He laughed harshly. 'You will not fool me! I know what you have been about, and who you sport with!'

'I am at a loss to understand you. What do you think you know of me?'

'I know, I have had you watched these many months, and have seen the evil men who have come to you in the dark of night! You are a harlot, yet you strive to appear virtuous. But you cannot fool me!'

'You are mad, imagining these things. Are you responsible for having me locked up here? I had thought better of you, Mr. Denham, and I do not think you repay me well for all the hospitality I have given you, welcoming you to my house so many times. What will people think when they hear what you have done to me?'

'You deserve all that you get! I have watched you, many a night, flaunting yourself before those men, tantalising them with your looks, your beauty, and your immodest dress!'

'Mr. Denham, I have never dressed so! Come, sir, you shame me to so accuse me, and do yourself harm to think so!'

'You wear bright colours and lace, and pull your gowns so tight so that your body is shown.'

'I do not consider bright colours and

lace sinful, sir, for even the Protector wears such. As for the other, would you have me wear a sack? I am not ashamed of my body, for God gave it to me!' she retorted angrily.

'But not to use it to torment me!' he cried, and threw himself onto a settle, where he rocked to and fro in agony.

Cherry looked on, growing understanding in her eyes. She had no false modesty about her effect on men, and had many times had to repulse too ardent approaches. She was aware most of the men she knew would have needed little encouragement to become her lovers, had she been so inclined. But she had misjudged Faithful Denham, assuming that though he admired her, he was so puritanical in his behaviour that he would not even think of her in such terms. Now she knew that he was eaten up with desire for her, and that this was at war with his creed.

She did not understand why this should have led him to treat her in such a way, unless it was futile revenge, or crazy jealousy, but she began rapidly to consider how she might use her knowledge to escape the trap. She sat down on a chair a little way from Faithful and considered him.

'Faithful,' she said gently, and he looked up, startled. 'May I call you so, for I think of you so, and you have been a faithful friend to me ever since my husband died.'

He stared at her, unsure of this new tone.

'Have you been thinking me so evil? Oh, my friend, I have been so remiss, so thoughtless!'

Still he did not speak.

'Is it true that I torment men by dressing so? Forgive me, I am a simple woman, and but young — my husband died so early, and I had no guidance from my family. Does it create disturbance in men? I love the bright flowers, and their colours, for they remind me of the country where I was so happy as a child. I dress in colours to remind me.

Am I wrong? Please tell me, guide me, for you are an experienced man, and I know I can trust you.'

'Yes, you are but a child,' he said slowly. She kept her eyes lowered to hide the laughter in them.

'What have you accused me of? They were terrible words that you used.'

'What was I to think?' he cried, holding his head in anguish.

'What of? I do not understand!' she protested.

'I had men posted, watching your house,' he said, each word dragging slowly out of him. 'They saw men leaving you late at night.'

'Who did they see?' she asked, a slight quiver in her voice.

'Dick Ashford, and John Taunton, and another I did not know until last week, Miles Talbot.'

'But they stayed to give me advice,' she protested. 'I am a woman on my own, I have great wealth to administer, and I needed help.'

'I could be better qualified to give

that than they! I am a merchant, but what are they? Pampered soldiers and friends of Cromwell! He does not value the right men!'

'You would have helped me? Oh, if I had but known! But many times I have wished to ask your advice and thought you too busy with your own business, for that is vast.'

'Yes indeed, but I would have been delighted to help you. But what of Talbot? What is he? How does he help you?'

'Why, he is seeking for an estate, and because he travels round the country, he has brought me messages from my mother, and my brother, and also been looking for suitable properties I might buy. There are, as you know, many that belonged to the rebels for sale, and as he was looking for himself, he looked for me too. We have spent hours looking at plans he has drawn up, until my head reels!'

'He is planning to wed,' he said, looking at her suddenly.

'Why yes,' she managed to answer without a pause. 'He has told me of her, and she sounds delightful, just the right girl for him!'

'Then he does not mean to wed you?' he asked in a tight voice.

'Faithful! What gave you that idea?'

'I thought, when I heard that he was to wed, and had heard also that he left your house so late, that it was you!'

'Oh, how can you think I deal with men in this sinful way? How long have you suspected me?'

He put his head in his hands and wept.

'I know not what to believe! We are told to beware of Eve, for she is false and leads men astray!'

'What have you accused me of? Faithful, I am frightened!'

He looked up at her, a cunning look in his face.

'Do you swear to me that I am wrong? Can I trust you?'

'I am not what you think me!' she answered indignantly. 'If, that is, the soldiers spoke truth when they came to arrest me. Have you truly accused me of adultery and of — oh, Faithful I blush to even think of it!'

'I could think nought else! I was so angry and you tormented me so!'

'I did not mean to hurt you. But I am afraid of what they will do to me. Can you not tell them that you were mistaken?'

'Are you attempting to use me?' he demanded, suddenly suspicious.

'You put me here,' she whispered. 'You must get me out. I have no one else to depend on. I shall die if I am forced to stay here in fear for much longer!'

'I will cancel the charges,' he said slowly, looking firmly at her, 'if you will agree to wed me.'

She looked at him in surprise. 'Why, I did not know, I — oh, Faithful!'

'Why are you surprised?'

'I had not thought of you a married man,' she said simply. 'I thought you despised such weaknesses of the flesh.'

'I do, but they are not forbidden, and better we control them in lawful union than lead others into sin. You need to be controlled and guided, and I have decided to take you as my wife. I will withdraw the charges if you agree.'

'I had not thought to marry again,' she said to give herself time to think.

'I have not thought of it at all until these last few months. You will be safe from temptation under my roof.'

'But Faithful, if you are willing to wed me, you cannot believe those charges you made. To save my suffering, withdraw them. I beg of you!'

'Not until you agree. I have wrestled with my thoughts and come to see that 'tis my duty to save you, and I am determined to give you no loophole to go back to your dangerous ways. When you have agreed, and not before, I will withdraw the charges. If you fail to agree, then I shall know that you are guiltier than you would have me believe, and you will be punished. I will have no more to do with you. I will have to admit that I have been a failure in my attempt to save you.'

'I cannot decide so important a thing so suddenly, for as I told you, I did not think to wed again. Please, will you give me time to become accustomed to the idea before I commit myself?'

He hesitated, but she stretched out her hand and laid it appealingly on his arm, and he shuddered, clasping it with his own.

'Very well. I will return tomorrow.'

Abruptly, as if afraid of her, he stood up and left the room, and she collapsed onto her chair half laughing, half crying at the thought of the man so pathetically lusting after her and so unwilling to recognise it, cloaking it with pious phrases, and turning his lust into a work he was doing for the sake of his God.

Soon she sobered, and began to think of the situation. She was unsure of the power Faithful had as her accuser, and soon rang to beg for an interview with the Governor. She told him that there was some doubt on the part of her accuser, who may have misunderstood some things he had seen.

'If he withdraws the charges, can he place them again later?' she asked.

'I doubt if he would have any reason to do that.'

'But if he did? I could not rest easy if I thought that at any time I could be rearrested on these horrible charges!'

'No magistrate would listen to him a second time. They would have to be new charges.'

'I see, that relieves my mind greatly. I thank you.'

The Governor bowed, and seemed prepared to stay, but Cherry smiled dismissal, and reluctantly he withdrew. She thought over the situation, and decided that in order to escape her plight she would have to pretend to Faithful that she would agree to his proposal. She would repudiate it later when she was free and safe from the charges. She had no compunction at using him so after what he had done to her, and no obligation to keep a promise extorted by force.

When Faithful arrived the next day, therefore, she smiled shyly in welcome and held out her hand to him.

'Well, Mistress? Have you decided?'

'Aye, Faithful. I had not thought to wed again, as I told you, but since you want me so much, I would be wrong to refuse you.'

He had been certain that she would agree, for she could escape the charges no other way, but he was so over-whelmed to hear her saying so that for some moments he could do nothing but stare at her. She looked back calmly and unsmiling. Then, with a choking cry, he moved towards her, and took her in his arms.

Cherry was tall, and he only just matched her height. He was elderly, thin and gaunt, but had a wiry strength. She flinched at his nearness, but he did not notice, and kissed her on the lips. She closed her eyes and concentrated on restraining her instinctive revulsion as his wet lips covered hers. She stood rigidly, enduring his embrace, until his hand crept tentatively to her breast. Then she moved abruptly, breaking away from him.

'No, no, sir! Faithful, I am no bawd! What do you think to do?'

He looked at her, breathing deeply. She turned away to hide the distress and dislike in her face.

'Come, I am to take you away now,' he said harshly, and with relief she gathered together the few articles her housekeeper had brought her the previous day.

The Governor was there to bid her farewell, and for an instant she hesitated, half wishing to throw herself on his protection. But she controlled the impulse, unsure of what it might lead to. She had to get outside the prison, and then she could deal with Faithful.

In the street outside a coach was waiting, and Cherry allowed Faithful to help her into it. He stepped in after her and sat morosely as they drove along the streets, passing St. Paul's, and into Canning Street. Cherry was watching the familiar sights as though she had been shut away from them for months instead of barely more than a day. She saw her own house, and began to gather her things together as they drew nearer, but to her sudden fear, the coach did not stop.

'What is happening?' she asked sharply.

'I am taking you to my house, my dear,' Faithful answered calmly.

'Why?'

'I prefer to do so. You have suffered a great shock, and I wish to see that you recover from it properly.'

'I shall do that best in familiar surroundings,' she said angrily. 'Tell the man to stop!'

'No, you will come with me. I do not trust you, and I do not intend to allow you to escape the promise you made. Women are as serpents, and must be held fast to tame them.'

'I made my promise, but I will not be forced in this way,' she told him.

'We will see.'

They had reached the house where Faithful lived, and the coach stopped. Cherry wondered whether she could escape if she ran for freedom, but before she had decided to make the attempt, two burly men appeared at the door of the coach and pulled aside the curtain.

'Take her inside,' Faithful ordered, and they grasped Cherry's arms and pulled her, protesting, out of the coach. She looked round desperately, but there were few people about and none seemed interested in what was happening. She tried to scream, but found that one of her captors had been prepared, and clapped his hand over her mouth. Within seconds she was dragged inside the house, and taken to a room at the top.

Faithful followed them up, and when she had been thrown unceremoniously onto the small bed in a corner of the room, he looked down at her triumphantly.

'Now I have you! You thought to escape me, but you will not be able to repudiate your promise.'

'You are despicable, and I would no more think of wedding with you than with the lowest scum of the kennels,' she said furiously. 'How can you expect me to accept you when you treat me so scurvily?'

'You are unruly, and I mean to tame you. You have great beauty that has tormented me these many months, and I intend to make you pay for the temptations you have caused me. You will never again be the object of lascivious looks, for I shall keep you here until I have forced you to behave in a suitable manner.'

'I will never wed you after you have behaved so treacherously to me!' she stormed at him.

'Will you not?' He laughed. 'That is to be seen. In less than a week you will be crying for mercy, and willing to repent your sins. You will do all I ask.'

'You underrate my aversion to you,' she said.

'I will leave you now to your reflections. Do not think to escape, there will be a guard outside your door all the time. You cannot escape.'

At that he left the room, and the door was locked. Cherry sat down to consider her situation. It was unlikely that she could escape, but she might be able to bribe the guard to take a message for her. She had seen the admiring looks the two men had given her as they brought her up the stairs, and thought that they would be easy prey.

She had not considered Faithful's cunning, however, for she did not see the guards alone, and as Faithful kept the only key to the room on his person, and came himself whenever the door was unlocked, she was limited in what she could do. She had tried to hold a conversation with the guard through the locked door, but the next time

Faithful visited her he told her gloatingly that there was always one of his trusted servants outside the door with the guard, so that no private conversation was possible.

'You will not seduce them into betraying my trust,' he said. 'Now, have you considered whether you will obey me or do I have to show you that I mean to obtain obedience?'

She refused to speak, and he surveyed her grimly.

'You will be hurt, and you will submit in the end. Be humble and submit now.'

She would return no answer, and he left her. For two days he visited her mornings and evenings, but she refused to speak to him. For two days she was given nothing to eat, and only a small glass of water each day. On the third day that was omitted.

On the following morning when Faithful appeared, Cherry was beginning to weaken bodily, but her determination to resist him was as strong as ever, and she returned no sign that she heard him when he began to ask the same questions as he had asked every time he had seen her.

'Are you willing to make good your promise? Will you wed me willingly? Has your stubborn sinfulness been driven from you yet?'

Cherry made no sign, and he lost patience and came over to where she sat on a chair, and shook her roughly. She flung up her arm to shake him off, but he simply caught it and twisted it cruelly behind her. She bit her lips, dry and cracked from thirst, to prevent the cry of pain escaping from her.

'You are a wicked jade, but I will master you yet.'

He flung her from him and stalked out of the room, and Cherry sat nursing her arm, fighting to keep back the tears. By the time he came in the evening she was weak with her sufferings, for she had been four days without food, and two without water.

'Here, take this,' Faithful said as he walked over to her. She was lying on the bed, feeling too ill to sit up. He thrust a glass in front of her, and roughly putting his arm behind her, pulled her into a sitting position. Cherry saw the glass, and allowed him to hold it to her lips. She gulped a mouthful as he tilted it, and felt the cool wine trickling down her parched throat. She thankfully drank more, and it was only when the worst pangs of thirst were relieved that she tasted the wine.

She sat up suddenly, pushing Faithful away from her, and spilling what remained of the wine over her gown.

'What have you given me? Have you poisoned me? That was doctored wine!'

Faithful laughed. 'Not so, my dear, just a potion to make you more complaisant. It will have no bad effect on you, but you will do as I say, and when the magistrate comes here in the morning you will, in his presence, say the words that will bind you to me for ever.'

'You fiend! I will not do it! You cannot keep me a prisoner for ever. I will let the whole world know of your base and wicked treatment of me!'

'You will not be able to, my dear. You will, in the morning, be ready to do as I wish, and after that I shall have full control over you as my wife. I shall return soon to see how you do.'

He left the room, and Cherry could already feel her limbs becoming slack. She struggled across the room, and managed to force herself to vomit into the bucket, but she had taken enough of the wine for it to have some effect, especially in her starving condition.

Swaying dizzily, she managed to reach the small window set high in the wall, and pushed it open. It was far too small for her to attempt to escape through it, as she had discovered on the first day of her imprisonment, but the cool night air swept over her, and she breathed it in thankfully, wondering what else she might do to ward off the effects of the drug Faithful had tricked her into taking.

She walked up and down the small

room, very unsteadily, for she was very dizzy, but with an idea that if she kept moving she would be less likely to succumb to the drug. It was a tremendous effort, needing all her willpower and failing strength, but she kept doggedly walking up and down.

It was about two hours later that Faithful returned. The guard who accompanied him carried candles which he set down on the table before withdrawing. Cherry blinked in the sudden glow, for it had grown dark during the past hour. She was still trying to walk about the room, dazed and only half aware of what she was doing, and she stumbled as Faithful caught at her arm.

'Well, have you given in?'

'No, never,' she whispered with returning consciousness of her surroundings, and undiminished determination to resist.

He flung her from him, and she fell across the bed. He gestured to the guard, who left the room, and returned with a riding whip in his hand. Faithful took it, and jerked his head. The guard, with a half regretful look at Cherry, left the room and Faithful locked the door after him, then turned to Cherry who was watching him helplessly.

'I will tame you,' Faithful declared. He seized Cherry's gown and tore it viciously. She tried to prevent him, but she was too weak to hinder him, and he had soon torn all her clothes from her. With a smile of satisfaction he stood for a moment gloating at her lovely body, then picked up the whip, and struck her with it across the legs. She gasped with pain, but did not cry out. He then brought the whip down on her stomach and again on her breasts. She cried out at that, and rolled over to shield herself, and he laughed with glee at this first sign of weakness that he had been able to drag from her. Again the whip was raised, and he struck her several times across her back. She had clenched her teeth onto the pillow and managed to avoid crying out, but she could not prevent the shudders that racked her body as the whip descended time after time.

The sight of her smooth flesh marred with the lashes from the whip, the luscious curves of her body, her long slender limbs, drove Faithful on until he was scarcely capable of realising what he did. Suddenly he put down the whip, and with an animal cry began to tear off his own clothes. Cherry realised dimly that he had ceased to beat her, and looked up fearfully. He was struggling to rid himself of his breeches, and she saw with revulsion his scrawny naked body. She also saw the whip he had discarded lying at the end of the bed, and tried to crawl towards it. But he was free of his clothes, and came at her, knocking the whip out of her feeble grasp.

She was weak, and he was stronger than normal because of his lust and madness. He pushed her back onto the bed, and although she found a desperate strength to try and fight him off, she could do little. Soon he was able to fling himself on top of her, grunting with a mixture of triumph and pleasure. As he fumbled with her she made a last attempt to throw him off, then, realising the futility of it, screamed in anguish, and almost lost her senses.

It was with utter incomprehension that she suddenly felt his weight lifted from her, and for a few moments she lay inert. Then the sounds of movement in the room roused her and she turned her head towards the sound. Faithful was cowering in a corner, while a man was belabouring him furiously. With a cry of joy, Cherry saw that it was Miles, and she struggled to sit up. Then she realised that there were more sounds coming from the stairs outside, but before she could distinguish what these were, another man appeared in the doorway. Dimly she saw that it was Dick Ashford.

At that moment Miles turned from the thoroughly cowed Faithful, and both he and Dick stepped towards her.

With a great effort she stood up and took a step towards Miles, holding her hands out to him.

'Miles, my love!' she managed to say before he caught her to him, and she collapsed into a flood of tears.

Gently he soothed her, murmuring endearments, while Dick looked on in wry sympathy. Then Miles glanced at Dick.

'Can you find a robe or a cloak? One of the maids.'

Dick nodded, and left the room, to return within a few moments with a cloak. Miles gently wrapped Cherry in it, and stood up with her in his arms.

'I will carry her home. 'Tis not far.'

'What of this sorry crew?' Dick asked, indicating Faithful, who was moaning with pain as he lay on the floor.

'He will cause no more harm, he will be too afraid. If you do,' Miles went on, turning to the cringing fellow, 'I will have you thrown out of the Company, and your chance of importance and your livelihood will be gone, and you will no more be respected by the Saints!'

He turned away, and carried the semi conscious girl down the stairs and out of the house. It was dark, and the streets were deserted. It took only a few minutes to reach Cherry's house, and Miles was soon laying her gently on her own bed. The housekeeper was hovering anxiously.

'Some soothing balm, and warm water, then wine and broth,' Miles ordered, and when these had been brought, he proceeded to bathe the weals on Cherry's body, and cover them with ointment. Dick gave what help he could, while the housekeeper hurried away to supervise the preparation of a meal. Cherry recovered somewhat under his gentle administrations, and when he had finished, and wrapped her in a silk robe, she was able to sit up in bed and take the broth.

Miles sat beside her, and insisted on feeding her himself, though she weakly protested that she was able to feed herself.

'You will allow me,' he said firmly, and she was too shaken by her experiences to argue.

After a while she was feeling surprisingly better, and smiled at them with a little of her old gaiety.

'Why do you not bring a table in here and eat while you tell me how you discovered me?' she suggested.

'You are not fit for talk,' Miles protested.

'I must. Please, my dear, do as I ask?'

Reluctantly he agreed, and soon they were all three sitting on the bed, the men eating heartily, and Cherry nibbling the wing of a chicken.

'How did you find where I was?' she asked.

'I have just arrived back in London, and called to see if there was word from you. I thought you would still be in Norfolk,' Miles explained. 'I found Dick here, also newly back in town, talking with your housekeeper who was most concerned about you. She told us how you had been arrested, and how you had left the prison with Denham, but been heard of no more. We came straight to his house, and were immediately suspicious because of the villainous looking fellow who opened the door to us and tried to prevent our entering. We had to insist.'

'Insist?' Dick laughed. 'If that is what you call it! He knocked the fellow out cold, and then fought his way through a gang of servants.'

'A rabble, they offered no resistance,' Miles said drily.

'Then he found another armed man on the stairs, and was dealing with him when he heard you scream. I have never seen a man move so fast. He pushed the man out of the way, and calmly ordered me to deal with him while he broke the door down. By the time I had finished off what he had begun with this guard fellow, he was beating the life out of Denham.'

Cherry shuddered. 'Thank God you

came, my love, for I could not have fought him off any longer! He had drugged me, after starving me for four days,' she explained, and Miles' eyes grew dark with anger.

'All this, to have his way with you?' he asked.

'No, I do not think he intended that, but was carried away. He said that 'twas to force me to wed him.'

Dick laughed. 'The old goat! So he had some red blood in him after all! Poor Cherry!'

'I will kill him if he dares to lay a finger on you again!' Miles declared slowly.

Dick raised his eyebrows. 'And you, my friend? Cherry has found a worthy champion.'

'You would have done as much for her,' Miles said, smiling at him.

'Aye, but she had eyes for no one but you. You are a fortunate fellow. May I congratulate you.'

'Dick, Miles and I are to be married.' Cherry said, holding out her hand to him. He took it and held it gently, looking affectionately at her.

'He is the most fortunate man alive. I wish it could have been me.'

'You will stay our friend?'

'Of course, and be glad to. I could not tear myself away completely from the enchanting Cherry! But now, 'twould be tactful of me to leave. May I come to the wedding?'

'Dick, you are a dear! Kiss me farewell.'

With a mischievous look at Miles, Dick complied, lingering as long as he could, until Cherry laughingly pushed him away.

'Take care, Miles is a jealous lover.'

'But 'tis my last chance, I must make the most on't.'

With a gay wave of the hand, he left them, and Miles held Cherry gently. 'I will never leave you again, to get into such pickles,' he said, half jokingly.

'I am safe now.'

'Will you go to Flanders when we are wed, and await me?'

'No, my dear. We have work to do. I must go to Norfolk and discover who this man Cotes is, and you, I imagine, have new instructions?'

'Aye, but I cannot bear the thought of your being in danger.'

'I will not be, for we will be together. Will you come to Norfolk with me?'

He laughed. 'Aye, when these cuts are healed, and we are safely wed, we will journey round the country together. If you cannot drum up support for the King, no one will be able to!'

'And we are still undiscovered here. I can go on working amongst the Parliament men.'

'Not in the same way as before.'

'No,' she agreed. 'I will reserve my wiles for you in the future!'